SECOND WIND

CAUGHT BETWEEN PAYCHECK AND PASSION

SANCHIT GUPTA

olive turtle

NIYOGI BOOKS

Published by
NIYOGI BOOKS
Block D, Building No. 77,
Okhla Industrial Area, Phase-I,
New Delhi-110 020, INDIA
Tel: 91-11-26816301, 26818960
Email: niyogibooks@gmail.com
Website: www.niyogibooksindia.com

Editor: Keerti Ramachandra
Design: Shashi Bhushan Prasad/Cover: Misha Oberoi

ISBN: 978-93-86906-96-0
Publication: 2019

Printed at: Niyogi Offset Pvt. Ltd., New Delhi, India

I sulked and grieved in the cage I was bound

Lo behold! Until I found,

The chains I curse have never been there

The bars are golden, the feeds are rare

Lounging on the floor, staring at the sky

Longing to fly,

If Only

I Could Try

To everyone, who has a dream

CONTENTS

PART III

THE CALLING CARD

It was the month of April and I had just gone home after finishing my MBA, a welcome break before joining work.

'How are the preparations going?' I asked Vivek, as I lay on my bed, staring at the roof. We had surrendered ourselves to the benevolence of our desert cooler that was busy sprinkling tiny droplets of water on our parched faces.

'It's fine. Physics and Maths are good,' he replied. 'I am facing some trouble in chemistry though.' Vivek was my cousin, a student of standard XII preparing for the IIT entrance test, the sixth person in our family to do so.

'Hmm. Good. Keep it up.' I said, 'Do have a plan-B in place as well. IIT is not the end of the world.'

I knew the significance of having a plan B. My plan-A had failed twice.

'Yeah, I don't have any such qualms,' he said, 'in fact, as I see it, engineering by itself is not the end of the world for me.'

'I see. Then what is the end of the world for my young brother?' I asked, trying to dig out the secrets he had hidden away.

'IIT I am preparing for because if I get through everyone will applaud me since no one in our family has been able to crack it yet. Mummy would be proud of me. But if you ask me honestly, I want to become a rock star.'

Wooooohhhhhh. That was a bolt from the blue. ROCKSTAR? I knew he played the keyboard, or would sometimes sing a few numbers and post the videos on YouTube, but seriously, from where did he get such a weird idea? The kid still lives in a dream world, I thought.

'You should look for a career which also matches your competencies,' I offered my unsolicited advice. 'I have seen the world outside, and it's full of exceptional talent. Competition is extremely stiff. Only someone rare, born under lucky stars makes it big, others are doomed to oblivion. And then even daily life becomes a struggle and fulfilling basic necessities becomes a challenge.'

'Yes, you are right, easier said than done. It would demand a lot of sacrifices,' he said. Good, the boy isn't that stupid, I thought. 'But bhaiyya,' he turned towards me, there was restlessness on his face, '*kuch bhi ho, kuch legacy to chhodni hai.*'

Six years ago when I was in Class XII, I had the same spark he had in his eyes that day. '*Kuch legacy toh chhodni hai,*', I used to say. Six years later, I advise people to remain grounded, to have goals that are realistic and not harbor impractical dreams.

Why?

PART I

THE INSPIRATION

"Success, it is said, is 99% perspiration and 1% inspiration. Perspiration we all do, but where do we get that 1% inspiration from?"

READY TO RUN

I was a blessed man

'Take it all in.'

I was not Karan's girlfriend so I didn't know what he meant. His eyes shone as if he'd just had a Eureka moment, like good old Archimedes in the bathtub. He took out his crisply ironed handkerchief, cleaned the mustard stain off his red tie, tucked it back in and buttoned up the blazer. He placed the now crumpled handkerchief into his bag and pulled out another. He picked up two vodka shots and held them high above his head as if cheering me on, like a king exhorting his subjects.

'Why don't you just take the tie off?' I took the shot and asked him. I hated those snakes of silk floating around my neck, but I could see he loved his, so refrained from any more comment. I wondered if he had taken offence at my suggestion. He said nothing. Would he have walked away if we'd been anywhere else in the world? This was a new city, I was his colleague, both of us were in our first jobs since passing out of college and like me, he too knew no one else in the organization. In a sense, I had been thrust upon him. I was his forced friend, if that is a kind, and we had to stick together like birds of a feather that flocked together. Was that why he'd remained silent?

And then, without preamble, he declared, 'It's a process Sanjay,' emphasizing the word 'process.'

'What is?' I asked puzzled.

'We worked on the Three Horizon model today, right?'

'Yes we did.'

'The Chairman gives these speeches every year about the future of our legendary organization and we have to distil it and present the greatness of those ideas to Baap tomorrow, don't we?'

'Yes we do.'

'Doesn't that excite you?'

It was kind of okay, I would have said if I'd been pushed to spell it out. Because honestly, I thought this was Baap's way of getting the new management trainees out of his hair because he didn't know of anything better for them to do. Of course I couldn't tell Karan that. He was acting like Neil Armstrong prepping to land on the moon next morning.

'Yes it does.' I said trying to bring some enthusiasm into my voice to match the sparkle in his eyes.

'So when we present tomorrow, I assume it's going to be *we* unless you chicken out, right?' I don't remember why he nudged me as he chuckled. 'We need to be prepared to be at our best. You know what can happen when it comes to Baap.'

We had heard rumours. I didn't, however, wish to ruminate on them at the moment and ruin my happy evening.

'So, are you preparing for tomorrow's presentation, as we speak?'

'Oh yes, my friend!' He pulled back his sleeve and shook his wrist to roll his watch out. 'It's two Karans you see in front of you right now. One who is having shots with you, the external Karan. And the one rehearsing the presentation for tomorrow, the internal Karan. And Booba knows they are both killing it real.'

I didn't know what Booba was and I didn't ask. I tried to guess but I couldn't, so decided to keep quiet. What I can say, though, is that when I witnessed the confidence and charisma in Karan that night, I was convinced that I was lucky to share the table with him, and the prospect of growing a career alongside him.

Karan got up and went back to the bar. He was quite a generous fellow I figured as he cleared the tab for both our drinks and didn't ask for a split. He had a wife called gallantry maybe, for he didn't even give me a chance to insist. I thought he wanted to see himself as an elder brother, the one who knew how things went while the naïve kid bro didn't. I thought how cool it would be to have him as a real elder brother. I too might have gone to him a few years ago just as my younger brother had come to me. I might have told him about the first lead I'd played in the theatrical performance presented by the theatre group I had formed in college, and wondered if I could keep running it forever instead of joining IOC. I knew exactly what Karan would have done to me then.

He came back to our table with two more shots.

'Karannnnn!' The words lingered in my head before I let them out, 'IOC is not your first job, isn't it? Second one right? So you must be having a plan or something for what lies ahead?'

'Of course,' he declared, 'excel in every role the organization entrusts me with. You know the big O that's called Outstanding? Promotion in three years, salary doubles in five. Then jump off the ship with a 50% hike. Every goddamn HR in the country would want to snap me up.'

I couldn't help myself. I imagined a giant with the words HR written on his t-shirt snapping Karan between his fingers.

'That sounds good,' I said.

'It sounds great man, just listen.' He clinked the two shots together and we took them both in. 'Doesn't that sound great?'

I nodded. 'It sounds about right.'

'What about you? You have a rock-star plan?'

He was like my history teacher – asking tough questions, making me scramble for answers. I hadn't thought of this question for a long while. 'Do FMCG marketing maybe,' I said, 'that's why I came here I think, and then see what next.'

'I would say just bank the money my friend, you hear me? You are not going to chicken out tomorrow, are you? Booba knows Baap will kill us both if you do.'

I couldn't hold myself back. I had to ask him. Both his brother and father were head-honchos in two multinationals so I believed he would know the answer.

'Tell me something Karan,' I almost begged, 'tell me very honestly, are you really ready to run the race?'

'What race?'

'Nothing,' I said. Clearly he and I were not on the same page. 'I will wake you up at 7:30, and you can lend me one of your ties.'

We got home drunk that night. I didn't know whether I was happy or sad. I set the alarm for 6:30 am the next day, a day which I knew would dictate my life from here on. What I also knew, however, was that unlike Karan I was not an IIT/IIM person, a species revered in this country, on the presumption that they held a passport to success and for which every kid in our 250 million households were given training. I was a 'second rung premier b-school' graduate, the silver medalist who manages the podium but not the million dollar endorsements, the second topper who studies as much but doesn't get featured in the school honor board. There was only one person every year from my institute lucky enough to get into IOC and all four hundred and twenty of us vied for that golden spot. Raised in a middle class family, I had no family inheritances or hidden sources of income to boast of, so a 'good job' was next only to God in the pecking order. Being happy or sad didn't matter, being there with Karan that night meant I was a blessed man.

Yes sir, I am ready, I am ready to run the race.

THE BAAP

Don't worry, we will reimburse your auto fares

IOC Ltd, or Indian Oriental Corporation was a great Indian conglomerate that sold nearly everything from packaging cartons to beauty soaps to luxury hotels. With offices across the globe and more than thirty thousand employees swiping their access cards every day into its hallowed chambers, it was a dream organization to work for. Especially for the blue eyed B-school graduates like us who had been fed this dream since we were kids, when we couldn't even spell the word organization. Karan and I, the revered PPO (pre-placement offer) holders from our respective colleges had been assigned the enviable task of taking the 100-year-old glorious empire into an even more glorious future like the many hundreds and thousands had done before us.

One of those brave vanguards was Mr. S. Sundarajan, Board member of IOC Ltd. A mechanical engineer from IIT Kharagpur, he had joined the company in 1975 as a management trainee, just like us. Today he headed the Strategic Growth Division of IOC and was directly responsible for businesses worth Rs. 12000 crores.

It was he who was instrumental in growing the division from near scratch to the pinnacle of success it stood on today, and who five CEOs of five business units under the division reported to. A chain smoker, he was a state level tennis player in his prime, and so fit, that even today he could simply walk into

IIT KGP and walk out with the annual tournament trophy in his hands.

Talk to him about any topic under the sun and there was a high probability he could discourse on it. He had a colossal memory which seemed to have everything neatly stacked under well labeled compartments, shelves and rows like a gargantuan world library where information storage capacity was limitless. Where the microprocessor was so advanced that any minute scrap of data could be accessed with lightning speed, straight from the hard disk to the cache within nano seconds, which made me wonder if Intel must study the anatomy of his brain for the next technological breakthrough. Gifted with an uncanny ability to play around with words, he was a glib talker, and a persuasive orator. Even if God came to him one day for a possible confrontation, it was likely that the Almighty would be so completely enthralled by his arguments that He would agree with him. As for using technology to its maximum capacity, he could put any boastful youngster to shame, for right from his smartphone to the Mac, and video conferencing devices to Pinterest, he had mastered them all. He used them to keep us on his radar even when not in office.

So, even though he was meeting us for the first time today since we had joined, we had been constantly bombarded with tons of material to read, projects to undertake and agendas to learn. As the Hindi saying goes, not even a leaf could move in SGD without his permission. For us new *bachchas*, he was our boss, our HR, our mentor, our friend-philosopher-guide, the decision maker of our future. In short, Mr. S. Sundarajan was our *Mai Baap*.

'Good morning, sir, may we please come in?' asked Karan as the clock struck 9, right on the money.

'Ya, Good morning! Okay…Good…Go to the conference room, will you? Discuss amongst yourselves, look at some ways of presenting your learnings and I will join you in a moment!'

'Right sir, we shall do so, sir.' Karan's response was instant.

That's confidence. See how calmly he is talking to the big man, I thought. Will I ever be able to do that?

We went into the conference room and almost stopped short. A grand boardroom kind of table I had hitherto seen only in movies, fitted with a video conferencing unit and an array of microphones, a wall size screen projector and a whiteboard. Wow! This is where those big billion dollar decisions must be taken. I stood near the whiteboard and picked up a marker. You see, my dear friends, that is how we shall go on to acquire Visitas, our toughest competitor, a move that would make us the biggest conglomeration in the world. Congratulations! The audience struck dumb, wearing a look of admiration and incredulity, cheering, applauding, rushing up with compliments, newspapers and bulletins world over talking about the inking of this century's biggest acquisition. Millions of jubilant shareholders… Kudos!

It was 1 pm. Baap was still caught up with chhota baaps and allies, or other Baaps from other corporations, while we had been psycho-analyzing our grand presentation for the past four hours. We had spent uncountable attempts making exhaustive notes, digging through the Chairman's visionary speeches, to arrive at our own blue-eyed vision that must make and not break our first impression on Baap.

The plan was thus: As soon as Baap enters (and we hope he does), Karan and I will raise ourselves up and floor him with an unparalleled analysis and spectacular presentation which the legend would not have witnessed before. There would be questions of course. After all every presentation in college was invariably followed by some spooky questions which the pseudo classroom had to ask in order to earn bonus marks for class participation. That's when our two year MBA course would come in handy, for there we had learnt that any damn question on this earth can be answered with any damn answer on this earth, leaving the quizzer to connect the dots. The deadly duo of Karan and Sanjay was all set to mesmerize the oh-so-eulogized Baap.

About half an hour later he came in.

'Okay, Good. I am sorry you had to wait. Tell me, what have you done?'

We stood up, he sat down. We said our Good afternoons, No problem sir, We have been reading sir – whatever came to our suddenly shaken up minds. I looked at Karan, who was trying to put his words together, 'Sir, aaa…as you had said, we have been trying to analyze the Chairman's speeches through this Three Horizon model, a…aa…aand, as we see in 1996, we had decided to step up on our tea exports…'

'Okay, good. Who is the number one exporter of tea?'

Pin drop silence. It was not in the speeches, hence not in my notes and the presentation.

'I didn't ask you to not find out, did I? He, he, he! So have a look at that,' he stood up with a marker in his hand, 'and also at other exporters. What is the market size for tea?'

Not in the speeches either. Another silence.

'Find out about Sri Lanka, US, Brazil and China. What do they grow? What kind of tea? Now I am not asking you to do a biotechnological research but you should at least have a fair idea of the product you are talking about! Had I asked you to not find out?' Another chuckle. 'Who produces it, where? How many people do we employ?' He fixed his gaze on Karan, as if interrogating him in a murder trial. 'Mmmmm, many farmers sir.'

'How many? Are they all as rich as you, Mr. Indian Institute of Management from Bangalore? We need to look at the other India too, which stands under the sun to plough those farms as you and I sit in this air conditioned room sipping coffee and making fancy presentations.'

A collective chill went down our spines.

'So have a look at that. Go to the internet, find out, take some magazines from my office, read about the industry. And while you are doing so, visit some shopkeepers, find out how they sell things. Now I don't mean you go and tell a shopkeeper I am an MBA, *falaana-dhamkana*, and hurl a volley of data at him with your pie-charts and graphs. *Woh bolega, hato boss, abhi dhandha karne do.* He, he, he! Chat him up, make friends, observe how he is selling. Go to the factory, watch how the processing takes place. Meet people. You marketing guys can give suggestions on what needs to be done so that the engineers can plan the production. You see, we don't always need a classroom for learning, do we? Open your mind. Go do that, and don't worry, we will reimburse your auto fares!'

PAUSE. Long pause. Tick, tock, tick, tock... Some of the most excruciating seconds of my life. Should we say something or just keep mum?

Baap soon resolved our quandary. 'And what was our share price yesterday?'

Unfortunately, even that was not in the Chairman's speeches. 'Sir, around 170?' I hazarded a guess.

'Don't guess if you don't know the answer. *Abhi tum shareholder ka paisa duba dega woh gaali humko dega!'* A big guffaw this time. I concealed my embarrassment and put up a fake smile. 'So do all this, and we will see you guys later.'

Any damn question on this earth cannot be answered by any damn answer on this earth, and if the quizzer is your boss, never make him connect the dots, or he will disconnect yours. I guess all those surveys were right after all! B-schools don't produce industry fit grads. To say the least, we had been thoroughly ripped apart and loaded with tonnages of work. I didn't show my pale yellow teeth again and Karan didn't utter his 'Booba' even in his dreams. There was a lot to do, and we could easily be put under another round of firing tomorrow.

Karan was right, I was naïve.

FINE BLACK PRINT

Hope is a dangerous thing

'80 m high and 82 m span, end to end, sir.'

'Does it have the stipulated check meter in place?' interrogated Karan.

'Yes sir. Show you sir, come, come.' And he took us both around the huge power generating edifice, behind a compound bounded by a barbed wire fence. Two identical electric meters were installed on either side. 'All statutory regulations sir, we follow. Put up since commissioning. No error, exact readings, sir.'

'And it is there in all five?' the tone had become sharper.

'Aaaa…in four till now, sir. R300, problem! What to do, we have been telling the electricity board since long. They just don't put up! These government people, very lousy, sir. Nothing happening unless you bribe. Corruption everywhere sir!'

'Hmm, it would be better if you get things done Mr. Pillai. Shareholders' money you see, can't take chances.'

It had been just two months into the system and one could already see Karan unleashing the boss within him, a privilege which, although rare as of now, would surely spring to the surface whenever he came across an ingratiating subordinate.

Mr. Ramakrishna Pillai, the site manager for the wind farm we owned (I had begun to use 'we' as a pronoun for IOC), was one such person. These windmills in Southern Tamil Nadu, to where we had flown Business Class for the first time in our lives, were ones which we at IOC had setup to enhance our renewable energy propaganda. They were erected by a vendor whom Mr. Pillai represented and to whom we had been sent as auditors. Baap never treated us as 'trainees'`. He believed in delegation to such an extent that if need arose we would be told one fine day to run SGD, but if and only if, we could prove ourselves worthy of doing so.

As 'auditors' (a word of which I didn't know the exact meaning even though I was supposed to be one) we went across each of our windmills, asked all relevant/irrelevant/ Baap relevant questions we could think of and clicked every action/inaction/Baap relevant action-inaction into a snapshot. Mr. Pillai took us to a decent restaurant nearby for lunch, which Karan thought was obligatory on Mr. Pillai and part of his job description as the ingratiatory, while I felt it should have been on us as a goodwill gesture from the ingratiated. Human elements of *'pehle aap'* are weighed on the scale of corporate appropriateness, said the obligation theory, and the practicality of the bill en-cashing on Mr. Pillai's company and not his pocket notwithstanding I learnt, while eating sambhar, rasam and pappadum on a banana leaf, the first lesson of my new world: *Human etiquette plays second fiddle to the nuances of corporate etiquette.*

'What miserable food and pathetic roads! We must ask for an extra TE for this trip,' said an apparently irritated Karan as we got back to our Innova.

'Can we do that?' I asked, 'Isn't there a fixed amount or something?'

'Of course we can,' Karan declared. 'A simple theory of give and take! It is the company's duty to squeeze out as much work as it can from us, and they do so, don't they? Hence, in return, it's not just our duty but also our right to maximize the moolah we can squeeze from them. A perfectly symbiotic relationship, nothing to be ashamed of! All you need is to learn the ways, that's all,' and he raised his hands in the air again, as if in the 'Cheers' more he would often go into, radiating an odd sense of victory.

'When we reach office tomorrow, Sunder sir might inform us about our postings. What do you think is in store?' I asked.

'What's the secret? There are openings in the printing and packaging division I know. Most probably both of us will be put there.'

'But...' I was somewhat perplexed by his nonchalant attitude. Did he know the policies of IOC? 'But I was taken in for a different unit, soaps you know, I think I'll be posted there.' My voice was tentative, almost tremulous.

'Haha, that is funny! You *think*? On what basis? Get real Sanjay, things can change, I don't think they have a vacancy right now. Take what you are getting.' The matter was closed.

Karan was nothing in the IOC chain of command and he definitely didn't have access to Baap's mind, but his comments left me worried. What if he *is* right? There was talk of the lack of vacancies doing the rounds. What if I do get printing and end up doing industrial sales? All through my MBA I had planned to make a career in FMCG consumer marketing, completed my education for that purpose, and now I simply let it go down the drain just because the company I joined asks me to? Is that fair? But what options do I have, a mere drop in the ocean of IOC, why would anyone even listen to me? What they say, I would have to do, that's what even the seniors have been saying all this time.

But then what about my hopes, my desires? What about the "do what you want to do" stuff they keep talking about? What about dreams? Just let them go? Find happiness in what is shoved down my throat?

Maybe I should start looking for a job somewhere else. Some other company which offers me the job profile I want. Yeah, as if that is so easy, you dumbass. And that too just two months after you joined IOC? Are you out of your fucking mind or what? The market won't appreciate that and your CV will get blemished. And who knows how the other place will turn out? By God's grace you have reached a place where others in your league could only dream of being in. Don't be so arrogant and let it go!

What about starting something of my own, as an entrepreneur? I have read such stories before, of IIM grads simply throwing away plush jobs they didn't like to do what they truly wanted to do! Maybe I can do that, I think.

Wow! You think? How ridiculous and foolishly over ambitious your thinking has become. You have never even had a job before, how can you ever run a company of your own? This isn't a fairytale, man, it's the real world, and the real world has real difficulties and real obstacles that you can't even imagine. You would never make it, trust me.

Then…maybe I can request a senior within IOC, that would be a good idea, won't it?

Come on, Sanjay, who are you kidding? Who would you go to above Baap? The buck stops there. Period.

That means I can do nothing? What about…

My head was swarming with questions I didn't have answers to. What could have been a casual comment for Karan had begun to play my past, present and future in front of my eyes, again and again and again. The taxi had reached the airport and we checked in. The business class did not seem classy anymore. It would be a long and anxious night I knew, and no matter how hard I shut the door, questions and doubts kept storming in. I switched off the lights hoping the stillness would anaesthetize the raucousness in my head. Let's wait for tomorrow, let's wait for the sun to shine again.

Hope, it is said, is a dangerous thing. I dearly hoped to see Karan being proved wrong. I hoped that night that the gods would look into my heart, and grant me a magnanimous tomorrow, when all that I wished for would be realized, that the path my life would take henceforth would be smooth and sweet as honey. I had hoped for a utopian world, the kind of comfortable world I had got used to in college.

When I went to office the next day, I hoped to walk into Baap's cabin and have him tell me what I wanted to hear. *Only* what I wanted to hear. Nothing more, nothing less. Not a word different from what I hoped for.

The clock struck ten and we were called in. He enquired about the trip we had been on and talked about our learnings and findings. He deliberated on various aspects related to wind, renewable energy generation, carbon credits, related environmental and business issues I should have paid attention to but didn't. My ears, eyes and brains were shrouded with hope that blocked the senses from performing their routine jobs effectively.

Half an hour passed and the discussion dragged on. I had no clue what was being talked about and was desperately hoping he wouldn't shoot me down with one of his rattling questions. Karan was nodding making intermittent interjections while I remained silent all the while. Baap's piercing gaze could shift to me at any moment and the slightest response from me could expose my ineptness. I was so terrified, I'd been mentally and physically crouching.

An hour passed and we were still in the discussion. He got up to draw some charts on the board, put down some figures and made a few crude flow diagrams. He had not mentioned a word I wanted to hear. I had fallen way behind in the dialogue he had initiated and was tired of hiding from his glances, feigning knowledge, but in truth, fretting about my posting.

I hoped the agony would soon come to an end and he would let us go. I had to pee. I hoped and I hoped and I hoped. I sat there like a statue clinging on to hope, waiting for a miracle to save my hopes from being crushed by another person's will, my ass being fired for being a non-responding clueless audience and my pants getting wet from the pressure of both. Honesty is a virtue I take pride in upholding so I will admit that I didn't wet my pants nor was I caught day dreaming. But I was the only hopeless act in the discussion during which the great man had expressed his hopes for a brighter future for the country and the company. Hope, I reiterate, is a dangerous thing.

By afternoon, Baap finally told us to leave and meet Mr. Senduvan, CEO of the printing business.

We had with us an A4 sheet of paper with fine black print on it which stated:

Welcome to IOC

We are delighted to inform you that as torchbearers of the future of IOC which looks upon you as visionaries and leaders of tomorrow, you are welcome aboard the Printing and Packaging business of one of its most distinguished arms, SGD. You are requested to meet Mr. R. Senduvan, CEO, Printing and Packaging, for the road ahead.

Regards

S.Sundarajan

My first reaction was curiosity. Why are letters like these signed by Baap himself? Is there no HR or what? Back in class, that's how they used to define the roles of Human Resource

– Recruitment, Training and Planning! What happened to the planning part? The second reaction was a furtive glance at Karan, who had his typical, '*See, I told you*' look on his face. I don't know whether he was happy or sad for me, maybe he wasn't bothered. What bothered me however was the look Mr. Senduvan gave us when we met him for the first time. Like a hungry vulture targets its innocent prey or an excited astrologer sizes up his hapless visitor, R. Senduvan's eyes too were peering beneath our upholstery and chassis, the engines that had now been parked in his garage.

I was doing my own assessing of Senduvan too. He must be in his late forties, I conjectured. Another IIM type of the bygone era, rarities in the outside world but a common commodity within. His manner was that of a man who knew his way around the world and its people, would talk straight and only as much as the person on the other side deserved. A man who demanded respect through fear of admonition wherever he went. It was no longer a mystery how a business with units spread across the most troubled regions of the country with the most disruptive labor unions were run so effectively. That he would brook no nonsense became apparent soon, for within a few minutes he threw the ball in our court.

'So, my young friends,' he said, 'what are you interested to work on?'

I knew very well he would not appreciate an honest answer from me, yet I blurted out.

'Sir, I am interested in a career in FMCG marketing.'

'That I don't have,' he shot back. An awkward silence ensued and my heart started pounding as if invaded by Godzilla. Karan nudged me to keep quiet, but I continued,

'Sir, that's what interests me the most. Developing communication and brand building…I have always wanted to do FMCG marketing. It excites me. Understand consumer insights and develop advertising to satisfy him…and…'

'If you don't satisfy the customer who has come to buy your packaging, he will kick you in the ass,' he smiled. 'My friend here thinks only making fancy ads with heroines is marketing, isn't it? I told you, I don't have that here. Is there anything else you want to say?'

Nobody in the room who sat on this side of the table spoke a word after that.

***

Later that afternoon we got back to our guest house to have lunch. While we had come to Chennai fearing sambhar chawal for years to come, the cook in our guest house must have been Gordon Ramsay's lost cousin. He could whip up any cuisine in the world with his special touch and would always have more dishes than an Indian shaadi's buffet waiting for us. While Karan loosened his belt to become Masterchef's judge again, my Gordon had been replaced by the Godzilla that had invaded me before.

'What's up Sanjay, why aren't you eating anything?' asked Karan, breaking my river of thoughts.

'Nothing' I said, 'just don't feel like eating.'

'Why? What's the problem?' It seemed he could read the lines on my face.

'Look Sanjay,' he continued, 'stop living in this dream world of yours. Things don't always happen the way you want them to. Stop being a kid and learn to accept what's given to you.'

'What does that mean Karan?' I shot back. 'I didn't spend twenty years of my life just to get a degree and do any given job. I spent it to do something that I actually love doing, something I really care about. You want me to let that go?'

'What else do you want to do? You read the fine black print. That is it, the company decides and you follow. Didn't you hear Sendu? Didn't he make it clear the first time? What were you trying to prove by arguing with him?'

'I was not trying to prove anything. I was only being honest.'

'O, *honest*! Didn't you see his reaction to your honesty? Don't you remember what the HR had told us a few weeks ago? You are a resource for the company and the company can utilize you wherever and howsoever they wish to. Period.'

I didn't know how to respond. He continued.

'Sanjay,' he explained, 'Sendu is your boss now, and you better accept it quickly. You offend him and things could become real difficult for you out here.'

I was quite peeved by now.

'You want to tell me that I shouldn't say anything? Just accept what is given to me and work like a donkey?' I snapped.

'There is no point, I am telling you. Do you think I would like working there?' Though we never admitted it, both of us feared that this might happen. Neither of us wanted to be in the division we had been posted in. Every time we met a senior we'd asked the same question, and were given the same answer – A change in division is impossible at this stage. Something like it has never happened before in IOC. 'You know my father and my brother,' he continued, 'I have seen the corporate world. At least do what you are told for three-four years, prove yourself through your performance. Until then no one will even listen to you.'

'Perform in what they want me to perform where I want to perform?' I snapped back, 'isn't it a simple choice Karan, pursue your own dreams or fulfill the dreams of others? Then why did we even get these fancy degrees and go to the so called good institutes? Just to earn good money? Oh, I have a better idea.

Why not go and open a *kapde ki dukaan* outside our homes and sit on the *galla*. There's real good money in that I tell you, even more than what our bosses' salaries are. And I am sure it doesn't need an IIT or an IIM degree to do so. Let's do that. What's the fuss all about?'?'

Karan sighed in exasperation. Had he given up on me?

'Do whatever you want. But remember, he is my boss as well. If you want to screw yourself, do it, but don't drag me down with you.'

PRIDE AND FEAR

Comfort zone – the enemy of ambition

'Day Zero Company dude, whatta lucky chap you are. *Career ban gaya Sanjay tera, ab to tu aish kar bas!*'

'Congratulations young man, IOC is a dream company for everyone, and in this time of recession, you have hit a real jackpot. Don't you forget my lectures there!'

'Wow sir, it's a real honor to meet you. Please guide us also on how should we prepare for our interviews next year.'

'Your son is going to IOC? You must be a very proud father.'

My father was indeed a very proud man. He would talk about me wherever he would go, to friends, peers and relatives. No one in our family had been fortunate enough to obtain this level of education, join such renowned an organization, or earn such a fat paycheck before me. The three magical letters, IOC, lit up the eyes of the listeners and made them look at me with hitherto missing awe and admiration.

Being a Management Trainee with IOC was like wearing a Cap that announced I belong to the elite league. I had fallen in love with everything that came my way – status, money, recognition. Love had grown into commitment, and even before entering the relationship, I had planned for a long lasting marriage.

As days passed, we started working in the printing unit we had been posted to. About an hour away from the city, it was one of the oldest properties owned by IOC, sprawling across acres of warehouses, machines and godowns.

Not far from the entrance and not too deep into the campus was the marketing office, where Karan and I were dispatched. The room was air conditioned, people were nice and the work was challenging. Within a week I got accustomed to the place. The work profile is not even that bad, so what if I am not designing advertising campaigns? I will still be doing production plans or negotiating quotations! It's true that I had not really aspired to do this all my life but then a truly happy person is one who finds happiness in what life gives him, isn't it? That's what I should try to do. After all, I am being paid well and there is job security in a tough market. Learn to be contented with what God has provided. It is my fate and I must embrace it gracefully.

Now, it's not that I didn't try to change it. I did go to Baap and told him about my interest. I put forth my plea politely. He is a great man, he would know what is best for me. He says it doesn't matter what kind of job you do, all jobs are important. What you need to do is give your full commitment to it. And then he gave me an assurance that he would transfer me after a year. I won't lie. I was disappointed. But what else could I do? It is true that I don't idolize my bosses here. And after a lifetime of hard and smart work, I don't want to become another Senduvan heading a printing unit. If anything, I want to work in FMCG marketing or run an ad agency or own a theatre group and production house where great ideas and plays are conceived, nurtured, produced and showcased every day! Certainly not making production plans for a living!!!

Let me not delude myself any longer. I have dreams but I don't have courage, and my confusion is a reflection of the fear I live in. I want to live a life I can be proud of but I am not brave enough to chart my own path. I had given Karan a pompous sounding speech on pursuing dreams and 'doing what you want to do', but I am too damn weak and too damn afraid to put those words into action.

The truth is although I did mention to Mr. Senduvan what I would like to do, I don't have the confidence or the conviction to talk to Baap about what I aspire to be. When everyone has warned me that it's not possible to persuade him, why try to beard the lion? What if my audacity annoys him and he fires me? I have already managed to dive into the bad books of Senduvan. Discretion is the better part of valor. I must not forget that I, a non IIT non IIM candidate have made an entry into the elite league, earned the Cap with great difficulty. Lose this job and I have nothing else.

Also, what if I am not good enough for what I aspire to do? What if I write poor jingles or my venture flounders? What if I fail? One can keep trying but trying does not make a living! How am I going to make both ends meet? How pathetic it will be to live on a subsistence salary when I have a very generous job in my hand right now. I know people in good posts in several great organizations. I have talked to them as well. Their advice is to stay grounded. They say I have not seen the world, and hence must not run after insubstantial dreams. Karan was right, there is no point trying to ask for a change. Stay with printing and packaging and do the best I can…

Having entered into matrimony with IOC, a honeymoon must follow—in the form of colorful days of the training period. An army man gets trained to defend his country, a doctor gets trained to save lives, an engineer gets trained to create the future, while a management trainee gets trained to know nothing but make everyone believe he is their boss. The core objective of this training program is to teach him the art of doing nothing but showing the world that the weight of the universe lies on his shoulders. I, therefore, undertake to outline some of the key features of the management training programme we were put through:

1. How to make simple things complex and easy tasks difficult.
2. Fudge data to concoct results – essentially become good story tellers.
3. A master's course in office politics.
4. Acquire the knack of staying back in office even when there is no work.
5. Master the art of shouting at your subordinates and continuously making them feel inferior to yourself.
6. Learn addition/multiplication in Microsoft Excel and set borders in Word.
7. Make animated presentations to impress the boss and make him think you are a genius.
8. And one of the most critical ones – Develop an optimum sized 'Fake Smile/Laugh' to be used at critical moments during interaction with the boss: like when he cracks a stupid joke, a client jettisons his wife's bad temper on you, or drinking at an official cocktail party.

The list above is not comprehensive. It captures only high priority action points. The rest, the trainee needs to observe and pick up from his peers and seniors. For which it is imperative that he is a quick learner. These are strict guidelines reiterated time and again during reviews and unless the trainee has internalized them and incorporated them into his character, he is not eligible to become a manager.

I was trying hard to keep up with the rigorous regimen. In a very short time, Karan became quite an expert in KE No. 4 and KE No. 8 and was seldom seen around. It left me alone for those long and idle hours after work in the tranquil residential park, away from the bustling city.

'May I please sit here?' The silence was broken by an unknown voice one day when I was having my lunch.

'Sure,' I replied as I continued to eat.

'Thank you, sir.' Sir, he'd said to me? I looked up at him. A young lad, must be a newbie. His soft voice and self-conscious manner was a contrast to his radiant face and a well-groomed appearance. Probably belongs to a well-to-do family, and is well educated, I conjectured. His demeanor commanded respect.

'I don't think I have seen you around. Have you recently joined here?'

'Yes sir. Actually I am currently a trainee, for a supervisor's role.'

Supervisor? A trainee for supervisor? That is like three levels below me! He must have noticed the condescending look I flashed at him. It was quite strange I thought, that unlike other supervisors he seemed much more refined in appearance and manner. It didn't make a lot of sense. Appearances can be deceptive.

'I am Sanjay, a Management Trainee here.' I disclosed *my* identity now and waited for that customary look of awe and admiration.

'Nice. I am Vishwant. I too am an MBA,' he replied.

Whaaaaaat???? An MBA? *You too are an MBA?* Then what are you doing being a supervisor? I almost blurted out.

'I completed my PG this year only from RMT College, Bangalore. You might not have heard of it.'

He was right. I had not heard of the college. Must be a dumbo I thought, couldn't get to a good college like me, hence in such a lowly profile. I threw him another disdainful look.

'I too passed out this year only,' I said, trying my best not to make him feel any more inferior than he already was. 'You like your job here?'

'It's all right. I am happy to do what I can.'

There was something different in the boy's voice. It didn't have the usual anxiety a newbie would have. It didn't feel like he was looking to impress anyone. He is just a supervisor, I thought, he should be terrified of me. Who knows I might take umbrage and give him a bad appraisal? Why does he seem so unaffected? Maybe he has a rich dad and he does not care. Then why does he need to work in a lowly post here?

I was confused as he continued. 'I have been fully into music all along. During graduation, a few of us decided to set up a band but things fell apart. So I did an MBA alongside to get a job.'

Alongside? You did an MBA *alongside* of music? People do music alongside of MBA you jerk, that's how it is supposed to be, I felt like ridiculing him. The perfect occasion to apply KE No. 5.

'So, that means you plan to leave soon?'

'No, not leave. I will continue in the job, and keep working on my band. I have set up a mixing studio at home, but it has its limitations. Home does not have much space for all the equipment, you know.'

A home studio? That's awesome. He must really be a rich man's son!

'So, aaa… What do your parents do?' I could no longer restrain myself. As sudden and as inappropriately timed the question was, it should have been his turn to take umbrage, instead he continued calmly as before.

'Dad works in a bank while mom stays at home. I have a younger sister as well. Dad has given me freedom. He says you can do whatever you want. Still, I didn't want to be a burden on him, so I took this job. The band won't happen overnight.

It may even take years. I will keep working here till something substantial happens. If not the band, I'll try and come up solo. I have been working on a few pieces for some years now. Hopefully I get lucky and draw in some sponsors some day.'

It was my turn now to give him a look of awe and admiration. You really plan to come up solo? And for that you are willing to work as a supervisor? This was getting too much for me.

'But Vishwant, how can you be so sure your solo will be a hit, yaar?' I asked in a patronizing tone and with a concerned look, 'I don't want to discourage you, but hypothetically, if it fails, what are you going to do then? To be honest, as a supervisor, your financial state might just remain hand to mouth. Have you thought of that?'

'I know, but it's okay,' he said, 'I will manage. It's not that the pay doesn't allow me subsistence, in fact I will still be richer than half of the Indian population, won't I? Anyway, what's the use of living if I have to spend my life doing what someone orders me to do? I might not succeed, but at least I won't have any regrets. And most importantly, I wouldn't at all mind struggling for it, maybe even for a lifetime. But I want to give myself a chance.'

'You could have gone to a better college and taken a better job,' I persisted. 'What was the harm in that? You would have been much better placed with a lot less risk. It's not that only you have dreams, I too want to write, stage plays, maybe start a theatre group. But I decided to first take up the best opportunity I got from college, work in FMCG, to be in what I felt is a reputed yet related industry, learn and take things as they come. Today, I am earning well and can still do what I want to. Isn't that a better way?'

'Could be, I never said it is not. It's not that I dream of starting a band, no, that's not what I dream of. All I dream of is making music. Maybe for myself, maybe for someone who would want to listen to it. But tell me one thing Sanjay, if you decided to be in the related FMCG industry as you say, what are you doing here in packaging sales?'

I wanted to tell him it's not that simple, but I could not. I wanted to logically prove to him that I am right and he is going on a path that has no future, but I could not. I searched for words but couldn't come up with anything. He came up with one.

'You have come into your comfort zone, haven't you? Secure job, attractive paycheck, easy work hours. A comfortable life. Now things here look okay to you, so you have stopped thinking about what you originally wanted. Comfort zone is the enemy of ambition. You are there, I am not. I will try. I might even fail miserably, but you won't even try. And that is why I don't feel sorry I didn't take that path you talk about. I wanted education but not for the purpose of getting a great job and earning good money. So I am fine with what I have. We have only one life, Sanjay and time flies by. You won't even know when you grow old, and one day you'll wake up and realize, Oh! There was a time when I wanted to start a theatre group, maybe I should have tried. That day, sir, you might regret getting this high paying job.'

That day and that hour, Vishwant was earning less than one-fourth the salary I was drawing and was three levels junior to me. Going by where he had started, it would take him a minimum of ten years to climb up the ladder and reach where I was sitting pretty at his age. Being the newbie trainee, he used to get bullied and ragged by almost everyone in the plant. Yet nothing seemed to affect him. I know many people who were brilliant and had joined great organizations at senior positions, who had thought they would be successful in their lives, and I wish they are, in all their endeavors, but on that day and that hour, I realized that out of all the people I knew, Vishwant was the only one who was out of the rat race.

THE ENCOUNTER

You say as if you have a plan

The fan was rotating at a moderate speed above my head. It made a strange sound as if complaining about being suspended from the ceiling for so long.

Maybe it wanted to get down and walk out into the garden. Open itself to the breeze and absorb the freshness that had evaded it for years. Reach out for the stars that freckled the sky, and illuminated the heavens, stretch itself into the universe that knew no beginning, no end. Reach for the stars, said the card which I held in my hands as I picked up the trophy for topping the school yet again. The teachers were all proud of me, the friends jealous. The boy is a prodigy, he is going to go places someday, they all said. Reach for the stars, Sanjay, a bright future beckons you.

The fan was still grinding itself out overhead making me even more restless. Vishwant was right. I have come into my comfort zone. Time will fly and one day I will be lying on my bed just like I am doing today waiting for things to happen, taking life as it comes. And I shall remain where I am, confused and afraid.

Vishwant is nothing, just a supervisor, why do I want to be like him? He might very well fail in his endeavors and be forced to lead a life of hardship. So why do I still envy him? What am I living for, just to follow the boss's orders every day? Go like a donkey and come like a donkey. He is living for his dreams, he his living for a purpose. No, it can't go on like this. I have to get up and take stock of my life. I have to go meet Baap again, implore, beseech, beg. What if he brushes me off, it won't be worse than where Vishwant is, will it? If he can follow his heart, even I can. I have to give myself a chance.

I decided to go beard the lion in his den. Are you really sure about it, asked Karan. I don't know, but I know I have to go. Maybe try one last time. Hmm… If you are going, go prepared, he said. You know how good he is with words. Be prepared with all your answers. The bottom of the pyramid confronts the top of the pyramid, remain careful.

Being a student of engineering and management, I knew of a variety of tools one could use for mapping an exhaustive list of permutations and combinations for efficient process analysis and decision making. I picked up one of those to equip myself for the encounter.

The tool I utilized was a simple flow chart the first class of computer science in school had taught me. There were certain inputs, certain processes, certain decisions and in the end, certain outputs. Linking them all together were the flow lines. What was important here was to remember how to link the various boxes so that all possibilities are covered and a best case scenario arrived at.

I will begin with the input, the first sentence I will speak. The input is most critical, for the flow chart takes shape depending upon who reads first data into the program. If Baap draws first blood, I shall be the one responding throughout the game. Hence, it's essential that I start the conversation.

What could the possible responses to my opening statement be? Negative, affirmative, time wasting tactics or diplomatic circumvention – the most deadly and powerful. From what I have seen of Baap, he asserts himself in a friendly manner, so he won't want to be diplomatic first up. A direct negative won't suit his tactics and an affirmative is out of the question. Highest probability – he will link my opener to another topic where he can ground me and then come up with his opener, hence seizing control of the negotiation. My response here should be one that lets me stay in my loop, come what may and not get swayed by his words.

So I prepared various openers and connectors to keep throwing the topic back in. Once you get on track, the next response is a series of whys. Why this? Why not that? Why now? Why not later? Or a round of attempted humiliation – 'You can't do this?' 'You are being too naïve.' 'You are keeping yourself too limited.' 'That's not what we expect from you.'

If you come through here and your lifeline still exists, the last level to be cleared is the 'maybe later' syndrome. By now he has made an acknowledgement of what you seek, but he will try to give assurance and put it off for weeks or months, which might never come. That is where diplomatic circumventing is required from your side, to move in with the opening, keep meandering around it, pounce on an opportunity and control the game. Now he is trapped, he can't go back to the beginning of the loop, for that would negate his stature. He doesn't want to go forward either. You have to make sure he stands where he is and gives you an answer.

The encounter lasted half an hour. I got fired at, bled profusely but persisted. I kept pegging him back with connectors, answered all the Whys he didn't even ask, retaliated his humiliation card with 'I don't feel motivated there' or 'This is my passion and my dream' and timely diplomatic interventions like 'I know I might be naïve but this what I believe in' and the best of the lot 'You are my mentor and you know what is best for me.' Finally, I got an acknowledgement in the form of a thoughtful silence and an answer.

'Okay Sanjay,' he said, 'Go to the plant. Find out how various kinds of packaging is done, what are the packs we make, what is the methodology and the process involved in each. What are the printing technologies, what are the raw materials used, what should be used where and why? How is a costing process carried out? What is the cost at which we source and supply? What is the market size, who are our competitors, who are the major buyers, who could be threats or opportunities? Do this, and come back. Then we will see.'

My God! That was like working for a Ph D in the business. I bet even Sendu doesn't know all that! And even after I somehow manage to get all the information, you will see? What do you mean by *see*? Why don't you just hang me and be done for good? Why this waiting game in which you know who stands the best chance to win? He is really THE BAAP. Hats off, boss. As they say in Hindi, *sau sonar ki, ek luhar ki.* Why does everything have to be a dead end? I felt trapped and directionless, having nowhere to go. It was a Saturday and I decided to stay back in the city itself, when the phone rang up. It was Karan on the line.

'Heyyyy Sanjay, *kya kar raha hai bey*? Today evening, 'Singh is King', what say, book the tickets yaar. I will reach by six. *Aur haan*, book three tickets, there is a new MT who has joined today only, in finance. She too will come. *Chal* then, now get your bum off the bed and get us the tickets. Cya.'

I didn't want to meet Karan. When he hears what happened, he will have a good laugh, an 'I knew it' look. To top it all, he's getting some new MT along! The last thing I wanted was to be with some stranger, put on the artificial social face. After casting a million curses on Karan and the stranger, I went and booked the tickets, three of them as I had been instructed: Singh is King, 6:30 pm, Inox theatres, Chennai.

We skipped the formal introductions and charged into the darkened theatre, just in time to catch the star-cast since they came really late. Karan was sitting on my left while the stranger was on the right. Unfortunately, I had managed to get seats in the second row from the screen, and it was pretty uncomfortable. There was not enough leg space, I had to slouch to get a better view. Since there was no proper headrest, I had to sit up straight with my neck craned for the full three hours. A perfect, newly invented school punishment, I thought.

Although the long-legged girl dancing on the screen was extremely pretty, my mind kept wandering off. To Baap, to Sendu and to Vishwant. *I would enjoy struggling for it, maybe even for a lifetime.* I was struggling with a chair and wanted to call it quits. How can one struggle for a lifetime? And then to Karan sitting on the left, who had arranged himself in a rather peculiar posture, quite lost in the gyrations of the heroine. *I have seen the corporate world. At least sit quiet for three-four years until you get a chance to prove yourself, till then no one will even listen to you.*

I decided to close my eyes and go to sleep, but the stranger wouldn't allow me to. She seemed to suffer from acute gigglomania. She would be in splits after every five minutes, laughing at every inconsequential word and gesture that emanated from the 70mm screen.

She was not very tall, shoulder height to me, maybe, so she wasn't facing any leg room problems. As a matter of fact she seemed very well settled. I stole a couple of looks at her. She had a round face with chubby cheeks and there was a glow on her typically wheatish Indian complexion. The corners of her small almond shaped eyes arched into the curved eyebrows that sheltered them. Her shoulder length hair was tied up in a high ponytail, yet a few strands escaped the rubberband and framed her face giving it a soft and ethereal silhouette. Her giggles accentuated the large and deep dimples lending them an endearing charm. She was dressed like most young women – in a pair of jeans, a tucked in t-shirt and sneakers. Suddenly she turned to me and whispered in my ear, 'What did she just say?'

'Unh...what, who, where?' Shaken by the unexpected query and guilty of furtively watching her, I stammered.

'Arrey, in the movie, what did she say? I just missed the dialogue.'

'I...I, I don't know. I missed it too.' Uff. Narrow escape. Hopefully she hadn't noticed.

She smiled. 'What are you doing if not watching the film? It's so funny!' She turned away and came back in a flash. 'Sorry, didn't even introduce myself. Raagini Malhotra.'

'Me, Sanjay Saklani,' I muttered. She smiled, and then had another attack of gigglomania. She had one of the most beautiful smiles I had ever seen.

We took the train on the way back. It was not rush hour, so we got seats easily. Karan and I sat opposite each other by the window while Raagini sat next to Karan. The city had just been lashed by an evening storm, and now a cool breeze was blowing on our faces. After a few moments Karan came straight to the point.

'What did Baap say?'

I told him what had happened.

'Hmm...' He thought for a few minutes before responding, 'You know what he is doing, right?'

I didn't know how to answer that question, so kept quiet. He continued.

'You hadn't told Sendu you were coming to the city, had you? He was enquiring about you.'

His words didn't sound too comforting. 'No, I thought meeting Baap was also official.'

'You think a lot,' he paused, and sighed. 'It's been two weeks since you joined the plant. Learning is all right, but you haven't taken up any real project yet. I hope you realize that.'

I did realize that. But I didn't know what to do about it. 'I don't want to Karan,' I said, 'you know that,' I snapped.

'Ha, you say it as if you have a plan,' he said, dismissively, making a mockery of every ounce of my self-esteem. I felt humiliated. But I couldn't blame him. I was the one who had been a cribber, not a doer. I was tense, insecure and lost. I couldn't look him in the eye. But involuntarily, my words came out. 'I do... I do have a plan. One week, and I will do everything he has asked me to do. EVERYTHING. And I will go back. Let me see what he *sees* then. At least he has given me something to look forward to, no matter how far-fetched. I can't turn back now Karan. I have to make it happen.'

I had no idea in the world how I was going to fulfil the improbable promise I had made partly to Karan, but more to myself. It was a dark night and there was no silver lining I could see amongst the clouds. What I could see from the corner of my eye was a derisive smile appearing on Karan's face. I couldn't say what he was thinking. Maybe he took me as too foolish for his consideration. No one spoke. There was tension in the air, and all three of us could feel it. Raagini had been listening to the conversation but hadn't stepped in. She must have been feeling unnecessary embroiled in the argument, I thought.

'Don't worry, Sanjay,' minutes later, she broke the drowning silence, 'I am sorry I don't know what exactly you guys are talking about, but if you really want it from all your heart, I am sure you would get it.'

UNCERTAINITY

If you are walking through hell, keep walking

The sun was setting on the horizon. Monday was nearing its dusk. Workers from this shift would gather around the nearby tea-stall for an evening chat, waiting to pass on the baton to those in the next shift. The show would go on.

Officers would lock their cabins and walk towards their cars. At the gates the security guard would raise his hand and place it on the forehead, a salaam to his saab driving by. Saab unfortunately is too busy to look at him; he doesn't have the time to acknowledge his gesture. It's already 8:15, it would take an hour if not more to reach home. Even if the sedan has a strong A/C, driving in traffic is taxing. A quick dinner followed by the 10 o'clock news. Children are saying good night, they must go to bed in time, get up in time, reach school in time, do their homework in time. Study well and become successful like their daddy one day. The client was not too happy, boss has given a deadline. If we can't remove the defect in the next shipment, we might lose the contract. A big loss won't be accepted, warnings have come from the top management. Heads might roll. I have cracked a new supplier, a plan has been proposed. Have to work out the numbers. Tomorrow morning itself. How much ROI can we maintain? Shall also take him to the Taj in the afternoon, these firangs like the Taj. Honey, I am going to sleep. How long will you take? The clock strikes 11:45, one more report and we should be done. The new Harry Potter has released. Kids have been pestering for so long. Will take them to the movies this weekend, finally some time off I hope, should mark it in the planner. Oh no! Coming Saturday? Have to be in Head Office! Mumbai. Quarterly presentation, might even get a promotion this time. We will go for movies next Sunday, or maybe the Sunday after that. Whenever. It's 12:30 am, should finish the report. The alarm clock I have bought is very punctual. Rings sharp at 7 every morning. Children are still sleeping, will catch them in the evening. Got to get ready and rush. Honey, you got your breakfast? Ya, will eat in the car. Feet on the pedals and hands eating the sandwich, knees controlling the wheel. It's a brand new day. Tuesday has met its dawn.

One-sixth of the week had gone by and I had only learnt 1% of what Baap had asked me to. I would go from person to person, asking questions and seeking explanations, surf through all the presentations and reports I could get hold of, hop over from machine to machine conversing with the workers. Everyone is so busy, how can I keep disturbing them? Half a day has flown by, I have only managed to learn about silk screening by now. Still not sure how these individual processes fit in the complete flow chart, need to try and catch some expert soon. It was time for the canteen, a place which served everyone from the worker to the CEO with equal diligence, with no preference or prejudice. Even though the menu wasn't too tempting, the cries from the stomach managed to pacify the imploring taste buds, just like their owners on whose tongues they rested, to adjust to circumstances and compromise in life.

'Costing you can leave to me, I'll teach you that, will also give you the latest figures,' said Raagini, some of her hair having managed to make its way out of the pony tail today as well. She took off the catcher, held it in her mouth and with both hands behind her head pulled all the hair back in place. I wanted to tell her not to do that, those wayward strands looked good when they strayed onto her face.

'Thanks,' I replied. 'Where is Karan, doesn't he want to have lunch?'

'He was going to Sendu's office he said. He says he has been idling for many days now, wants some project. Aren't you going to meet him as well?'

'I hope not, I try to keep as far away from Sendu as possible. Come on Raagini, if he catches me and hands over a project then I become accountable. I will be stuck here till that project gets over. And then who knows whether another opportunity will even present itself. That is why I have to get back to Baap in a week.'

'Ok, ok. Why do you start throwing a tantrum every time Sendu is mentioned? Relax, just use the week effectively,' and then she flashed that infectious smile, pointing her spoon towards me, 'and if you get through this, you give me a big treat, ok?'

I smiled back. I don't know whether I was responding to her or laughing at myself, and at the miniscule possibility of 'getting through'.

'Alright,' I said, 'If I get through this, I'll take you to Taj. A gentleman's promise.'

***

The weekend arrived sooner than I had wished, and I was not sure how much or how relevant the information I had managed to muster. Let's see: processes I have gone through them all, and with some confidence I can say which is to be used where and when. What advantages does one have over the other? I think I should be able to answer well there. But that is only theoretical knowledge, practically there might be several permutations and combinations. How can I internalize them without any experience? Costing methodology I have understood, memorized few major figures too, don't know if that suffices. Technologies, hmm... I have taken an overview, but as a marketing person how much detail do I need to go into? What else...threats and opportunities? I have jotted down a few but there could be innumerable threads to this topic, how am I supposed to cover everything?

This is worse than those vivas in college. There, at least we had some sort of a prescribed syllabus. Here, it is infinity. For every word I utter, he can hurl a million hostile questions at me. If he is anyway not going to change his mind and this is nothing but a tactic to squash me, I don't stand a chance. He has been in the business for thirty years and I have not even completed thirty days! He can hand me a Zero and very comfortably stamp me as undeserving, erasing any hopes of anything in the future as well. Gosh! I don't know what he is expecting from me, or if this is of any use at all! Anyways, all I know is that I had promised myself a week and I have done all that I could have in these seven days. It's not a time to panic, doesn't matter what he asks, I will go with whatever I have.

7 am. A beautiful Monday morning. The first thing I did was to turn the news on. Previous encounters had taught me that when you meet Baap you need to be prepared for everything. Everything. While you are regurgitating on offset printing, he might suddenly switch the channel and dive into politics in China or geography of Latin America... So what is the capital of Honduras? There is something out there which has direct implications for our plantations? I didn't ask you to not find out? Hehehe...I should at least be prepared with the day's headlines. He would rip me apart if I didn't know what was happening around the globe. After the news, I went for a walk around the apartment, shaved and put on the best set of clothes I owned. Though he was scheduled to come in at 9:30, I reached the conference hall by 9 itself. I was ready.

The building was empty and I might have been the first person to break in that morning. There they were again, an array of microphones perched on the table, the glass top reflecting your own self as you bowed over it. I used it to smooth my hair.

There was a stillness in the air, the proverbial calm before a storm. I could hear the saliva drying up inside the mouth, the fabric of my trousers brushing against the wood and the air gushing past the nostrils. I deliberately started taking deep breaths to keep the nerves under control. The clock ticked away the hours. 10, 11, 12. It was noon and I was still waiting. Maybe he doesn't want to see me today. A waste of a day. Sendu is bound to give me a good bashing once he finds out. I kept breathing deeply and browsing through the notes. I have the share price on my tongue tip today, I hope he asks. Still no signs of Baap. Sitting there alone with a million thoughts exploding my head and waiting. Doing nothing but waiting. Wait and wait and wait. I was exhausted.

Four hours and fifteen minutes after I had stepped into the room, he came in and asked me to leave. We'll sit after lunch, he said. I hope he has some meal plans for himself as well, unless I was on the menu. Finally, at 2 pm, began encounter no. 2.

'Ok...good...so you're all prepared?' I had put up a small presentation on the projector screen. As he looked at it, a slight smile flashed across his face. Gosh, I hope I don't over promise and under-deliver.

'Yes sir. I have here a presentation on the processes involved in the various packs we make. A black box model delineating the flow charts,' I said, trying to maintain eye-contact. 'The first process here is that of our tea pack. After procuring the board of 300 GSM which is used for this pack, the first step is the offset printing on the Heidelberg, so we make the plates for that.'

'What kind of plates?' he shot back.

What kind of plates? *What kind of a question is that?* There is no *kind* in plates! For all that I know, they are simply plates, printing plates.

'Sir, what kind...meaning?' I tried to garner more clues.

'Is it CMYK or RGB?'

'CMYK'. Hah, got it! I knew that!

'Why CMYK? Why not RGB?' he probed further.

Why CMYK? It's like they always used CMYK, is there also a *why* to it? All I had ever heard was that CMYK is the technology used for printing. Nobody ever told me *why* CMYK. And why is it even necessary to know that? Maybe it's simply that the process once began with CMYK because the inventor had his whims, and now it has become a part of the culture, I presumed. He had noticed the confusion on my face and was glaring at me. Something needs to be said, NOW.

'Sir, I think because it is being used for centuries so now only that is used everywhere.' Great job Sanjay, what a lame answer.

'Earlier I thought you knew something about the business but now I am sure you know nothing,' came back the derogatory reply.

The blood in my veins froze. The heart it seemed would stop beating. I felt as if I had inadvertently stepped on a snake in its hole.

'Go back to your optics. Read about additive and subtractive color technologies. Find out how colors and lights operate and the difference between a bucketful of ink and a Cathode Ray Tube.' He took out a cigarette, leaned back in his chair and barked, 'Continue.'

I felt as if my worst fears were coming true. He *was* going to shoo me away, no matter what. The weight of my whole body descended to my knees. I wanted to stop struggling and quit.

I felt my fingers unwilling to feel the laptop again, my voice begging to stop running against the tide but flow along the current, the brain imploring me to shut down. And to this day I remember, that against the gale that was meant to blow me away, it was my soul that held the fort, the nerves and veins bound to the shore of hope; the soul that gives one the strength to crush bricks even when the bones have become brittle, a strength latent within all of us, but yet undiscovered. If you are walking through hell, keep walking. It was the strength of my soul that day I remember, a strength which urged me to not surrender.

I stepped up to the plate and picked the most complicated process next. 'Now I move on to this liquor packet.' I said, trying to gain some confidence, 'A costly affair, it has a sheet gravure followed by a Heidelberg offset print. Then there is UV screening, silk screening and foil stamping on the designated areas.' I picked up the board to demonstrate what processes have been carried out on what parts.

'How is silk screening carried out?' he enquired.

I knew what the process was and what benefits could be derived from it but I hadn't gone through the technical specifications. Damn. 'I can guess, but I am not very sure,' I said, waiting for another round of reprimands. He kept silent. I continued, 'It helps us make patterns or designs. A silk screen opaque plate is used to conduct the process. It is passed through a UV light chamber to achieve the desired effect.'

'Why is the plate opaque and not transparent? You should have talked to the workers or engineers and clearly understood how the process is taking place. You did your engineering before coming into marketing right? What's the use of your being an engineer if you don't know this?'

I nodded but kept silent. I didn't want to reply. I could have found out what he had asked, but I had considered it outside the scope of my study. His unrelenting questions and scornful castigations seemed to merely bounce off my expressionless face. Suddenly and strangely though, the gale seemed to be abating into a moderate breeze.

'We mean well for you, young man, but we don't expect such naivety in your answers,' he said, sounding almost guilty for coming down too harshly on me. Then with a broad smile he got up, took a sheet of paper from the diary in front of him, and cut four holes out into it. Then he took another sheet of paper and placed it below the perforated sheet.

'This is the formation,' he demonstrated, 'the paper above is the screen mesh while the one below is the substrate. The mesh is in the form of the silk screen design we desire on the pack. The UV fluid is applied on the substrate. Now, can you apply some common sense?' he prodded me on.

'UV light I know polymerizes the UV fluid,' I said, trying to develop a hypothesis, 'so maybe when the whole formation is made to pass through a UV rays zone it polymerizes the fluid on areas where we need the design, while others are left in liquid form. After the plate is removed, the substrate is washed, the fluid drains away but is retained in the polymerized UV design form.'

Bingo! I had got that right. I could see an expression of 'finally, the boy gets it' on his face. For two hours thereon, the quizzing and discussion went on. I might have been able to answer only about 20% of his questions, 20% he might have answered himself and for the remaining 60%, he asked me to visit the plant again, spend some more weeks there and plug in the gaps. And what do we do after that? I wanted to ask, but couldn't muster the courage.

Uncertainty. Uncertainty. Uncertainty. If I leave the discussion here, I might not progress to where I wish to go.

As Karan would say, this could be a tactic to arouse in me an interest in the packaging sales profile, so that my resistance could be countered more easily.

It was a dark tunnel I was groping my way in, and no light could be seen at the end of it. Shouldn't I say to him, 'Yes sir, I will do what you say but this is not what I eventually want.' Then what about Sendu? If at the end of it all I remain stuck there and he happens to find out about my little adventure, he will leave no stone unturned to book my ticket to hell. I felt I was trying to sail in two boats at the same time, and would end up sinking to the bottom. The easiest task in the corporate world is for the boss to tell you what he wants, the toughest – for you to tell him what you want. Don't we all become lambs in front of our bosses, my boss in front of his, his boss in front of his boss' boss and the chain continues. After all, each one of us, no matter how big or small, be it a simple executive to a vice president, we are all at the mercy of the one who writes our appraisals.

As I was contemplating the next step he got up as if to close the meeting. I said my *thank yous* and he began walking towards the door. Now is the time Sanjay, now or never, do it, the heart was shouting at the top of its voice. 'Sir, I shall do all that you have asked,' I spoke up, trying to infuse some strength in my quivering voice, 'but along with that I was wondering…'

'What? Tell me,' he turned around and fixed his gaze on my anxious face. 'For any trivial matters you can contact my secretary.'

'No sir, actually…I was wondering…I had few ideas on our distribution strategies in FMCG,' I tried to devise a lead to where I wished to go, 'I was thinking if I could be given an opportunity to explore those…'

'I never said don't do it, did I?' back came the classic reply. I knew he was playing me, a study on sales and distribution was impossible without the support of the relevant team. I could have done something substantial only if I could get to work along with them, in the system. Anything from outside would only be a perfunctory view that could be swatted like a fly on a glass of milk.

'Would it be possible to work along with the system?' I asked. There it was, I had taken the plunge. This was another way of saying, 'Can you post me in FMCG?' Or, 'Will you give me what I want even when I know you plan otherwise?' I could see disbelief and amazement written all over his face. Clearly he wasn't expecting this. The question was the same I had raised a week ago, but this time the context and scenario were different. This time I was asking for something to prove myself, I was seeking an opportunity to do something credible on my own initiative, and that too while accepting and doing what he had asked me to do. It sounded more confident and self assured.

'No. If you want to do something there, do it yourself. But do what I have told you first. Now go back to the plant. We will meet up later.' His tone suggested that he had gauged the growth in my confidence and had taken guard. It must have suddenly dawned on him that the past one week and the two encounters he'd had with me had engendered a slight alteration in his attitude towards me and the views I wished to get addressed. As for me that was enough even if it were only a meager 5-10%. A five percent is better than a zero, even if it is way behind the hundred. Even if encounter no.2 had ended with me failing to answer 4 out of the 5 questions he asked, even though I was humiliated and mocked for the naivety and inadequacy I exhibited and even though he was unwilling to give me any leeway, I felt I had at least managed to take one small step in the journey that lay ahead of me.

RAAGINI MALHOTRA

I wanted to hold time in my hands

'What is this, Papa! Didi is always late getting ready. Why don't you say anything to her?' I was complaining to my father, stamping my feet impatiently. I wanted to show I was not going to let her get away with it. No more delays would be accepted.

'It's okay Sanjay. She'll be out in a minute. Now behave like a good boy,' he said, wagging his finger at me. Kids have an instant recognition of danger. I understood Papa too would not let it pass. He too meant business.

'But Papa, if we don't leave now we will miss the Lanka Dahan!' I wailed. My dad didn't like to see me cry, so finally had to give in. 'Okay,' he said, 'you go ahead with your Mummy. I will bring Didi with me.'

As soon as I got the green signal, I grabbed my mother's hand and urged her to go with me. Our house was situated near the river amongst the hills, in a small township called Rampur Bushehar in Himachal Pradesh. We made our way across several gullies lined with houses decorated with multi-colored rangolis, walls adorned with pictures of Gods cut out from old calendars, and leaf torans, strung on the gates as a sign of welcome. Children were running around the pathways that crisscrossed the mohalla. At a slightly higher altitude from the neighborhood lay a huge playground inside a school compound. Apart from being the students' paradise, it served as the venue for any big occasion in the town, like some bada babu's son's marriage, a helipad for the Chief Minister's helicopter, or the colorful annual *mela* during the much-awaited Ramlila.

Nestling in the Himalayas as it did, our town used to get really cold at this time of the year and our mother was very particular that we were properly dressed. She had bought two thick overcoats, one for me and the other for my sister, and only after we had worn a monkey cap and woollen socks would we be allowed to walk out of the house. Although I wouldn't admit it I loved the overcoat. It had two pockets on either side and I would fill them both with groundnuts to munch while watching the Ramlila. My sister too did the same. With our pockets full, we would go to the Ramlila ground every night. People would either stand or sit on the stone steps encircling the ground. I would make sure we got the best seats, in the center of the back rows so that those standing didn't obstruct our view. Our parents would be on either side of us. We would shell the groundnuts and put the shells back in the pocket so as not to litter the ground, while we watched Hanuman dance all over Lanka, turning the kingdom of evil into smoke and ashes with his fiery tail…

Sixteen years had passed by. The festive season was upon the country, and the nine day Navratra was being observed everywhere. Sitting in my cubicle as the sun set on one more mundane day, I couldn't see anything festive around me. I hadn't been to a Ramlila in years, ever since I left home. Maybe they no longer have it. People have watched it on TV so many times, why would they go to see an amateurish show put up by some kids? I wanted to ride a merry-go-around, play the hoopla, wheedle money out of my dad to buy me bright pink candyfloss, and a dhanush-baan, symbolizing Ram's bow and arrow, clutch the lottery tickets in my hand and wait for my name to be announced. Did the city have a large enough ground to organize a *mela*, I wondered. But then, who'd want to play the hoopla when there is X-Box in the home?

I was lost in my thoughts when Karan came in. 'Hey Sanjay, it's seven o'clock. What are you doing? Have you ever been to a dandiya?'

'No, I wanted to but never got a chance, or even the desired company,' I replied. That was a lie. The city I lived in earlier offered many opportunities, but the 'desired company' never came along.

'I have two passes, Taj Coromandel Dandiya and Dinner, Five Star! A supplier gave me, *ab tu to contacts banata nahin hai*.' Quintessential Karan, I thought, as he continued, 'I would have gone, but I have to visit home this weekend, something urgent. The passes are for Saturday, and don't you dare waste them. Get someone to go along.'

I had always felt such big five star parties are more tamasha, more of show and less of culture, so I wasn't too excited by the prospect. But then, I had nothing better to do, nor a family in Chennai to celebrate the occasion with. So without a second thought I asked Raagini if she would be interested in going with me.

'You said you wanted a party right? Well, I haven't got through but what I have got is two passes. To the Taj, no less. Dandiya and Dinner. Want to come?' I asked most casually.

'First of all,' she said, 'you haven't got through *yet*. No one knows what the future has in store so remain positive. And second of all, of course I'd love to come.' She smiled, snatching the passes from my hand. 'You think I would miss such an event?'

I had never been to a dandiya night before. I didn't know whether Raagini had or not, but in any case, I didn't want to come across as dumb. I hunted through my untidy almirah for the red kurta I had brought from home. Yeah, there it was, right at the back of the pile of clothes, a bit soiled but would look fine after a wash. What about footwear? It must be something that matches the attire and occasion. I went to a nearby shop and bought a pair of jootis. I didn't know at that time though, that the seemingly harmless jooti I had just bought would have unfortunate repercussions on my feet as the dandiya progressed.

The big conference hall within the hotel had been revamped for the night. Doors, windows and walls were festooned with flowers, green leafy creepers, wall hangings and various other artifacts of traditional décor that could now be easily sourced from modern retail. The large open space in the center had been left for the dancers and chairs had been lined up along the walls, for the tired ones to rest their feet or the lazy ones for *nayan sukh prapti* – obtaining vicarious pleasure from the colorful spectacle before them.

At one end of the hall was a stage with a live band performing folk songs. Men and women and boys and girls of all age groups and backgrounds tapped their feet and struck their sticks in unison, with a natural rhythm in their movements, lively energy in their actions and unbound ecstasy on their faces. The place had a quaint charm to it, a mixture of traditional and modern and I felt thankful to Karan for giving me the opportunity to be there that night. With of course the desired company.

Fortunately or unfortunately, Raagini too was a dandiya novice. We picked up our sticks from the heap near the stage and stood like dorks in middle of the floor, not knowing what to do. Raagini had chosen a green churidar for the night and a gold coloured kurti with embroidery around the neck and cuffs. *Chikankari* work I thought, in a floral design. The sneakers were gone and her little feet were nestled in small heeled sandals with golden straps. In contrast to the tomboyish image she normally presented, this occasion had brought out the lady in her. There was eyeliner and lipstick, long dangling earrings matching the lovely necklace with a glittering diamond pendant. For the first time since we'd met, her hair had been left open, the dark strands framing her glowing face. She kept pushing her hair behind the ears every now and then, but some rebellious locks kept escaping back to cover the eyes and cheeks, charmingly defiant.

'Excuse me,' she said, to a man passing by, 'we are new, can you please show us how to dandiya?' waving the colorful sticks above her head.

'It's simple. Follow the music and make a pattern. Here,' he took the sticks from me to demonstrate. 'In one beat, we hit the sticks with our right hand, next beat with the left and then both together. The next beat we miss, just dance. You see, hit, hit, hit and miss. Hit, hit, hit and miss,' and he started dancing with impunity, as if he was the partner of my desired company.

'Okay sir, thanks a lot,' I snatched my sticks back and announced to Raagini, 'I have learnt. Let's dandiya!'

'Take off your jootis, they will hurt your feet while dancing,' she suggested. 'No, no, no. I will be fine. Let's begin,' I replied. I know I wasn't trying to be macho but I wanted to begin right away, without wasting even a second. She however, didn't think so. She went to a corner and took off the sandals, tied her dupatta around the waist and trapped her hair in the catcher she had in her purse. After a few minutes she came back, 'Let's dandiya!'

We started off slowly trying to gauge the rhythm. Hit, hit, hit and miss. Hit, hit, hit and miss. Sometimes, our sticks would hit the hands instead of the sticks, sometimes they would fly all over the place without meeting their counterparts. She was enjoying the mistakes I was getting good at, and her gigglomania would escalate every time I got into a tangle. I was not at all embarrassed by my clumsy movements for I was busy watching her dance rather than focusing on my feet. Soon, we felt we had practiced enough to dive into deeper waters. We moved to the bigger dancing groups of tens and even twentys, trying to catch their steps and movements. We fell, made others fall, laughed and made others laugh. I soon got tired and plonked myself on a nearby chair. She however, was the Duracell pocket dynamo it seemed! She was totally immersed in the rhythm of the music and was jumping all over the place, from group to group, partner to partner, infecting everyone around with her vivacity. So pretty, so natural, so pure, so innocent, so calm, so composed, so lively, so vivid, so simple, so beautiful, so fascinating, so mesmerizing, so true, so honest, so right, so perfect. I wanted to hold time in my hands, not let that moment pass. I wanted to watch her dance the dandiya forever.

The dinner was an eclectic mix of offerings from around the Indian landscape, Gujarati cuisine being the most dominant. Mouth watering khammans, spicy combinations of bhels, chats and dahi-bhalle or the sweet surprise of srikhand...we embellished our plates with a little of all the goodness around us. It seemed she had a particular crush on khamman, for she had filled half her plate with squares of the delicacy and was blissfully gobbling them up.

'So,' she said, holding one piece in her hand while another was in her mouth, 'how are things at work? What was Baap's reaction?'

'Hmm,' I said wishing I knew the answer to that question. 'Can't say for sure. He does get a little friendly at times but not sure what that means. It's difficult to interpret his motives.'

'You seem really keen on FMCG,' she said breaking eye contact, as if making a comment on something she wasn't convinced about, 'as if that is the only thing you want to do.'

Her comment made me think. There are several times in life when we reach a fork in the road. Which one to take and which one to leave? It's not that the path we choose at a given moment is the one we have always wanted to walk on, or wish to traverse for the rest of our lives. But it's the best available path at that moment. And so with hope in our hearts, we set off, until another crossroad appears and we have to make a choice once again.

'I find it more interesting and hence I feel I can do better there.' I paused, before speaking again. 'It's not the only thing I want to do, but it's nearest to what I do best or what I love to do, and its safe.' She waited for me to finish. 'FMCG is not my calling card Raagini, it's my safety net.'

She was nodding as if to acknowledge my confusion. 'I know what you are saying. Maybe everyone has the same thoughts in their minds. Most of us spend our lives in the safety net, while only a very few pursue their calling card. A lot of us in fact, don't even know what our calling card is.'

It was a statement I knew was true but didn't want to comment on it. I was fighting with Baap to at least get the safety net, so pondering over the calling card now was out of the question. With thoughtful expressions on our faces we continued to eat. The jooti had taken its toll, and both my feet were hurting from the blisters it had left behind.

After a few minutes, she spoke. 'I heard you like to write, right? *Kuch sunao humein.*'

'Hah,' I laughed out loud, 'people often have that misconception.'

'Come on,' she insisted, 'recite something. A poem maybe? I am all ears.'

'Oo...kayy. What do you want to hear?' I asked.

'Anything,' she said, 'it's a beautiful night. I had a great time. Something on tonight? Anything in your kitty?'

'Hmm,' I thought for a second, and smiled, 'I will recite to you something afresh then. A toast to tonight? Give me five minutes.'

I took out a pen from my pocket and scribbled some words on the tissue paper kept nearby.

'Eight lines,' I said, 'dedicated to tonight.'

Tickily, tackily, ticksy toe
Take two sticks and make them four
Up in the air we jump with joy
Shake those legs, no don't be coy
The rhythm is yours, now pick up the pace
The clock stands still, it ain't no race
Heads are turning, eyes wide clear
The prettiest of all, you are my dear.

As I finished reciting the poem I could see her blushing. Discreet, coy, demure. A slight smile flickered across her face.

'It is beautiful,' she replied, 'short, sweet and perfect. And thanks for the compliment. You wrote this just now?'

'Pretty much,' I replied, 'I am glad you liked it.'

'I loved it,' she said, with a broad smile this time, 'Sanjay, I want to ask you something.'

'Sure,' I said, 'go ahead.'

'You sometimes speak of some theatrical kind of start-up, what is that?'

I looked into her eyes and smiled. 'I know what you want me to say,' I said, and raised my finger towards her, as if educating her on some wise and profound truth. 'I do think of that sometimes. But making a career and following your passion are two different things, aren't they? You can't make a career out of your calling card. In fact, you shouldn't, it's dangerous.' I remembered Vishwant and shrugged him away.

'So what does making a career mean to you?'

Another difficult question. Is she some kind of an interviewer or what?

'Look Raagini,' I said, trying to sound convincing. 'Right now I am in a position where I am fighting to at least get FMCG, and even there I don't see much chance of success. To be honest, I feel even after all my histrionics the fine black print is all that counts. All the games Baap engages me in are just to amuse me. It's good to hope but facts remain facts. Even you know the odds.' I was looking into her eyes trying to drive home a point. 'See, I do want to establish my theatrical start-up. I do, with all my heart. But…it's easy to dream Raagini, to make it a reality is a different story. It's true that I did it in college, but that is behind me now, and life is no longer that of a student. I need to be in Mumbai for that. How can I give up my job here? And what would I live on? Who knows if and when the theatre group would generate any income. So where will my pay check come from? I must think practically.'

Raagini didn't reply. She lowered her eyes and got back to her food, eating slowly. It seemed as if she wanted to urge me on but the moment ordained otherwise. I didn't want to continue that topic. Every time I thought about it, I would feel more confused and directionless. To be honest what I secretly wanted was for her to say that she too had been mesmerized by my red kurta and the great dandiya moves I had displayed that night. That she too wanted time to stand still and for us to be binging on khammans together just as we had done today, forever. That she had a house in Bombay for us to live in, where we could pool our income (no matter how big or small) to run our lives and I could pursue the dreams she was asking me to realize.

'You ask a lot questions,' I said to her. 'Tell me, what's *your* story? I really don't think I know much about you. Where do you come from? What do you want to do?'

'I belong to UP, settled now in Patna,' she said. 'My father is an IAS officer while my mother is a housewife. I have a younger brother. He studies in school, in standard eight.' I had known Raagini for more than two weeks now and we used to have lunch together but this was the first time I came to know about her family. Today, I wanted to know everything about her.

'And your likes or dislikes? What about education? Where all have you been?'

'Who is asking a lot of questions now, me or you, Mr. Saklani?' she said, with a little mischief in her voice. 'See, most of my life has been in a hostel. You know Patna na, not a very safe place. Even though my dad always had security around us, he didn't want me to study there. So I did nearly all my schooling from a boarding school in Dehradun. What else, I learnt Kathak and piano there. I love to act in plays and that is why I keep asking you about your start-up. Maybe one day I can be cast as a heroine in some production of yours! It's good to be friends with the director you know,' she said with a laugh.

'Wow, that's interesting' I said, 'great to know you have so many interests. And you love to act? What all have you done so far?'

'Some productions while in school and college, that's all. I was the President of the Dramatics club in our college, Mr. Entrepreneur. You are not the only big shot around!' she said, flashing that smile again.

'Haha,' I laughed, 'I never said I was. So great, wonderful to know this. Then you should also pursue your passions, don't give them up.' You will, of course, be my lead actor, the heroine, I wanted to say, but desisted. 'Hmm…,' she took a deep breath before speaking again. 'It's easy for you to say Sanjay,' she said sounding suddenly melancholic. 'My parents don't really appreciate me doing all that. Don't get me wrong, I love my parents and I don't want to do anything that makes them unhappy. They allowed me to do an MBA only if I took finance and then got a good office job. But after that, they want me to get married.'

A sudden change came over her tone and manner. The smile I had begun to associate her with was gone. Her eyes lost their sparkle, as if the joy within them had given way to some deep seated sadness. She looked like she wanted to say a million things but could not. She was looking at me with eyes that longed to find answers, and I longed to tell her that I wanted to make all her worries mine. I wanted to hold her in my arms, protect her, secure her all my life. I wanted to tell her that I would be there for her forever.

'I understand Raagini,' I said, trying to be neither too sympathetic nor too apathetic, 'you still don't know about your marriage, right? Who knows what the future has in store? Live in the moment.' I wanted to encourage her to keep the hope and good things would come along.

'Nothing is in store Sanjay,' she said, in an almost despairing tone. 'My parents have already found someone for me. A family friend's son. I have been asked to meet him but…but I don't really like him, he is not the kind of person I want to be with. But then, what options do I have?' She paused. 'I am so lively na Sanjay, everyone tells me they thought I would have a love marriage. But all that happens only in fairytales, not in real life. And it's only a matter of months, or maybe even weeks, before I have to give up this job to settle down with him. Leave alone theatre, I feel everything around me is over. I feel my life has come to an end.'

We took an auto on our way back. I put my arm around her to try and console her. I won't deny it, but what she said that day came as a rude shock to me. This was the girl I had dreamt about, who I had waited for all my life, someone God had sent to rescue my hopelessly lost soul and set it on track again. But here she was, destined to go away from me forever. I wanted to stop her, to tell her that her life had not come to an end, that she must have hope. But I didn't. She looked at me with longing in her eyes and I looked at her with silence in mine. I wanted to speak to her heart, but I didn't want to say anything or do anything that might cause trouble in her family. I didn't want to raise any hopes that might crash later. I felt helpless. It's best to forget her Sanjay, I told myself. She is never going to be yours, no matter what. Get rid of all feelings you have for her. They will hurt only you and no one else. She has come into your life to go away. That is the truth, accept it.

DAWN AND DUSK

If sometimes we don't get lost, there's a chance we may never find our way

'I have so much on my plate it feels like a buffet,' I was saying to Karan. I had spent a week more in the plant by now, and was interacting with the engineers and technicians most of the time. 'I have to find answers to the questions he had raised last time, anticipate what more questions he might ask the next time, and most importantly, I have to do a sales and distribution study by myself. I still don't know how I am going to go about it.'

'You really think something will come out of it?' he asked, not expecting a positive answer.

'I am not very hopeful,' I said, 'in fact, if I go by the current vacancy situation, it's a long shot. The organization needs a resource here more than anywhere else. But what I have with me today is at least an opportunity to prove myself, to put forth my case. And this time around, if I am somehow able to make a good report on the study I have taken up, I can also back my claim with some performance, no matter how small, isn't it?

'Hmm,' said Karan as he lit a cigarette, looking away as he took a puff. He looked serious, thoughtful. I couldn't really say what was going on in his mind , but for that moment I felt that for the first time since we had met, Karan today wanted to be in my shoes.

Just outside the factory premises was a grocery-juice-cigarette shop. Every day after lunch while Raagini went back to her work, Karan and I would go to Anna's serve-all hotspot.

It was a place where action never stopped. Since smoking had been banned inside the factory compound everyone from workers to officers, engineers and managers, came out at regular intervals to try and release their stress and pressure in puffs of smoke. Ongoing projects, approaching deadlines, abusing bosses, politics at work were some of the flavours of the conversation.

Dear old Anna, the owner of the shop would watch the happenings throughout the day. He would serve us the coldest drinks, never complain about giving change, tell us stories he had overheard all day long during cigarette conferences, and the pains and pleasures salesmen or customers would confide in him. He knew so much about the business by just observing everyone. He would tell us about what order taking or delivery frequency different companies were possibly operating on, schemes that they might be running, credit issues he was facing, the modifications he had to make to his shop to cope with the growing business, products that would sell and that wouldn't. He was like a text book of marketing strategy and consumer behavior, always.

One fine day, just out of curiosity, I clicked him and his shop into my phone, to remember him and his little grocery store.

On the way back we bumped into Sendu. Oh no, that's bad luck, I thought. What am I going to say to him?

'How's your honeymoon period going?' he asked, glaring at me.

'Going fine sir,' I did some rapid thinking before putting my words together. Should I be diplomatic or courageous? After a conspicuous yet natural pause, I let it out. 'Apart from understanding the systems and processes here, Sunder sir has also asked me to do a study in sales and distribution of our FMCG businesses.' What are you doing Sanjay? Treading into dangerous territory? He won't appreciate that at all, and Sunder sir has not asked you to do that, you asked him *if* you could do it. Don't try to double-play; you'll be the one trapped in the whirlpool.

'Ok, good. I will see you boys later.' He smiled and walked away, leaving Karan and me perplexed by his geniality.

'What was that all about?' I said to Karan. 'You think Baap had a word with him?'

'About what?'

'Was that a smile of acknowledgement or sarcasm? What do you think is going on?'

Karan was as clueless as I was. I was petrified of what Sendu might do, but I also knew that it was no longer the time to be afraid. One can't discover new oceans unless one has the courage to lose sight of the shore. No matter how rough the waters were, it was time to set sail.

I spent two more days in the plant gathering all the remaining information I could to complete my notes. Then, without informing Sendu, I moved to the city. It was a dangerous move, but I had no other option. I put trust on the last conversation I had with him and prayed things would fall in place. I wrote Baap an e-mail on my progress to keep him in the loop. I had to make sure I made the right moves. The purpose of going to the city was to study the market, but the big question that now stared me in the face was,

HOW?

Amongst a multitude of challenges, the most distinctive ones were:

1. Lack of Tamil literacy, the only language which the retailer in Chennai could communicate in.
2. Ignorance of the actual functioning of the sales system in the company.

3. Total absence of guidance. I was working without the support of the sales team, and hence had no clue on how to proceed.
4. Last but not the least, no means of transport. Had to depend on my stamina, and my two legs to traverse the city.

How I wished I could take myself back to those classes in school where the bespectacled teacher wearing a khadi kurta would come in with his *pothy* to enlighten me on Sanskrit. Though a great language, it could never be of use to me because no one I knew used it, except of course the revered astrologer opposite my house, whose job required him to discourse on the apparently extinct yet extant language. I wished that the astrologer who would take special joy in prophesizing about my non-existent future, had taken a look at my palms and gone over my *haathon ki rekha* as well, and predicted a stint in the Tamil country someday. It might have inspired my parents to teach me the language for the ominous future.

After a few days of struggle on the roads, I had with me a head full of thoughts and a sheet empty of words. The cup of coffee lying on the table was staring back at me. It, and the other four that had gone down my throat earlier in the day, wanted answers, demanding a reward for the effort they had put in to keep me awake for the past three hours. Tomorrow Baap is going to be here, and then off to Headquarters for a fortnight. Tomorrow is my last chance, but I don't yet have a clue about how to begin.

I was browsing through the folders on the laptop when I came across the picture of good old Anna's shop. I could remember what he used to say, the accolades he would bestow and complaints he would record. And I began to write, penning down everything I had experienced as of now: good, bad and ugly. I didn't care whether what I was writing was the right or the wrong thing to say, but I continued to write, from the heart and without an iota of fear. All the views, opinions or ideas I had, everything that my marketing oriented brain ever wanted to say, I put down on paper. I took a printout and filed it. Then I made a presentation, bold and candid, challenging the status quo, questioning some of the practices no one in the organization had dared to do. I feared the consequences, but it did not bother me any more. I looked up and my eyes fell on the calendar behind the desk. 'Necessity leaves the timid with no option but to be brave'. Hmmmm.

'Don't worry Sanjay' she had said, *'if you want it with all your heart, I am sure you will get it.'*

Baap was quieter than usual when I stood up to make my presentation. He asked me to take a seat but I politely refused. 'Thank you sir, I feel more confident when I speak standing up.'

And I spoke, with all the flair and fluency which had resurfaced after being buried for so long under a mountain of inhibition and trepidation. Today for the first time since I joined IOC, I felt free, like a bird flying into horizons unknown, into the vastness of the sky, higher and higher.

Reach for the stars, said the card which I had once held in my hands. No, I couldn't top the exam that day. The heavens didn't sing out my name, and the gods didn't come down to bless me with flowers in their hands. I could not top but I didn't even fail. I spoke and he listened, he questioned and I answered, he argued and I asserted. The usual banter he would display was missing that day, the loud guffaw was absent. And finally, with a contemplative yet decisive look on his face, he said, 'You can go get a training in FMCG, plan it yourself, and then we will see.'

There was a world around me, 99% of which was full of compromises, of suppressing dreams and pocketing ambitions, a life embroiled in the unending race for promotions or annual increments. As I looked at Karan, I could see he had forgotten he used to sing in those fests once with hundreds cheering him on. His days now passed in trying to figure out what might appease Sendu next. I too was a part of this world.

You can't make a career out of your calling card. In fact, you shouldn't, it's dangerous. I was in a cocoon and had decided to remain sheltered within its protective covering forever. But that's not what the laws of nature ordain for us. They demand that we shed the confining encumbrance and flutter away like an elegant butterfly. As Vishwant would say, *I would enjoy even struggling for it, maybe even for a lifetime.*

If sometimes we don't get lost, it's possible we may never find our way. No, I hadn't really got all that I desired but I felt I had found the way. I felt that no matter how tough or discouraging the circumstances, it is possible even without wearing the Cap, or not having anything to fall back on, to aspire and achieve. I had heard the phrase 'nothing is impossible' several times before but only today I realized what it really meant. I began to look beyond what my limited vision could see, I began to think that maybe it won't be that dangerous to maybe once live outside the safety net, to keep an eye on the calling card, for no matter how difficult the path might be, it is not impossible. The way might not be clear today, but if the goal is, the road constructs itself on the way. It's not just an old fashioned saying; the journey of a thousand miles *indeed* begins with a single step.

I had begun to dream again.

PART II

THE SAFETY NET

"It's tough living with a dream,
but then it's tough living anyway"

JAGDALPUR
Walk the markets

'Where to?' asked the man sitting beside me.

'Jagdalpur,' I replied, and went quiet, not intending to make a conversation.

'Why?' he questioned, as if it was an interview, his face full of curiosity. He was a large middle aged man with a thick moustache and round eyes. He held a long *lathi* in his hand. His right cheek boasted a huge mole, the size of my eyeball, I thought. His inquisitive manner made me a little uncomfortable.

'Work, have some work in Jagdalpur,' I said, unconsciously straightening up. I prodded my bag with my foot to bring it closer to my legs. Being the only one in the rickety 1950s bus wearing Levis and Nike, with an Ipod plugged into the ears, I couldn't help being suspicious.

'Hau,' he said in response and settled back on his seat. A few minutes later, he turned towards me again.

'Jagdalpur na, what…what work?'

I had heard earlier, through sources reliable and unreliable that when educated or well paid young company officials go to places like the ones I was going to, it was a common practice for the local folk to gag them, then by plea or power, marry them off to their beloved daughters. Whether it was rumor or fact, I had no intention of proving it true. Trying to sound firm and unintimidated, I gave a fake reply, 'Relatives, relatives in Jagdalpur. I coming from Raipur, have relatives in Jagdalpur.'

'Oh, ok, ok. Relatives, *chuttiyan hai naaaaa.* Good,' he said, with a broad grin on his face. The mole had spread itself to twice its size with the dimples that appeared in his cheeks. 'Be careful still,' he continued, placing his right hand on my shoulder, 'Naxalite area all this, don't get into trouble. Remain in home only.'

'Yes, thanks, I will,' I said, trying not to look him in the eye, 'I will take care.' I huddled into the seat, my backpack firmly gripped between the legs. I felt as if all eyes in the bus were on me, viewing me, perhaps as a prospective son-in-law. Though I was still single I did not care to offer myself at the altar of rural development. I took off the earplugs and stuffed them inside the bag, put my phone on silent mode lest it blared out *'Kaise batayein, kyun tujhko chahen'* by Atif Aslam, and inadvertently sent out some unintended signals. A few minutes later, the 1950s bus, which could have been overtaken by a man walking briskly alongside it, ground to a halt.

'Halka hoe lieyo maa' yelled the driver as everyone started getting down, converting the roadside paddy field into a natural urinal. There was a mud walled house behind the field, on the front wall of which was written with coal:

> *Yehi hamar nara ho*
> *Har ghar maa shauch hamara ho*
> (This is our slogan
> To have a toilet in every home)

On one side of the field was a comparatively large pond. A few naked young boys splashed around in the Olympic sized swimming pool in their backyard, while an equal number of big black buffaloes wallowed in the shallows at the opposite end. A few women were washing clothes, while others were scrubbing their utensils. I couldn't help but pray that this water would not be served to me or anyone who chose to eat at this place, with dinner later that night.

On our way to Jagdalpur, we had halted a few kilometers before Bastar, a town in southern Chattisgarh. Like every other town in the state, Jagdalpur too, as I later found out, promised three things – Ghadi Chowk, Agrasen Chowk and truckloads of dust. In local parlance though, the quaint little town was known as the Kashmir of Chattisgarh, thanks to its natural beauty. People came here to explore its rich offering of caves, forts and waterfalls. It was not just the town but the whole state was endowed with numerous forts or garhs, thirty six in all, to be precise, which gave the State its name when it was carved out of the once largest state of Madhya Pradesh.

The state lay claim to two major sites associated with Lord Rama's Vanvas, Chitrakoot and Panchavati. I couldn't help compare the great Lord's exile to my own six month vanvas which my organization had banished me to as part of my FMCG training program. I had heard earlier, when I was gearing up to be an MBA, that those who get to do sales in rural India as part of their management training stints go on to become CEOs. I was eager to begin this CEO portending ritual as soon as possible.

'Good Morning Sir. My name is Ramteke, and I am Salesman with IOC Foods division. I know good English,' said the person my distributor introduced me to, who I was supposed to spend the whole day with.

'Good Morning,' I replied.

'*Saab*, should we go to wholesale or retail?' he asked.

What difference will that make? I wondered. Ramteke had bright animated eyes and wildly gesticulating hands that tried to liven up his speech. The shiny bald pate reflected decades of experience, his submissive manner and glib speech suggested he was a good salesman. Being addressed as *saab* by someone twice by age was a new experience for me. He must have spent more years doing sales than the number of candles on my birthday cake last year. My distributor later told me that he was one of our star salesman. No target was too high for him, no order too big. He had impeccable control over the market. Every shopkeeper spoke highly of him and referred to him as Ramteke Ji. There were outlets which didn't care for what the distributor or company managers like me said but would jump over a wall for Ramteke.

Yet, even after twenty years of glorious work in the field he had stayed where he had started. There was no position for which he was considered eligible, no accreditation that could change his fortunes. At the end of the month he would walk home with an amount less than a fifth of what went into my pockets, a fresher just out of college who didn't know the abcd of sales. That day, for the first time since I entered the professional world, I realized the importance of education. I had the luxury of affording one and also the luxury to crib about the very luxury I had been blessed with. 'We will visit both,' I said, and sat pillion on his motorbike.

The Splendor he owned was gleaming. Obviously Ramteke was very proud of his vehicle and took good care of it. He rode it at a leisurely 50 kmph even on empty roads, confident and carefree, rather than cautious. I did not particularly relish the thought of spending the whole day in the Jagdalpur sun and my patience was wearing thin.

'Ramteke, *is se tez nahin chalti hai kya*?' I asked.

'*Isse tez chalti hai na saab*,' he replied with a small smile, and continued to drive at the same steady 50 kmph Every salesman in the region rides a Splendor, I was told by Ramteke. Not one of them would cross the 50 kmph mark. 'Saves petrol, saves money,' he explained. He was paid 50 bucks as conveyance allowance every day and a few tinkles here and there could throw the monthly family budget completely off the track. It was only my first day in the field and I had already learnt two valuable lessons – the importance of discipline and need for sensible driving.

The first few outlets he took me to were small kirana shops, like the provision stores in our neighborhood where I was sent to buy stuff as a kid. The difference this time around was that at every shop I walked into, Ramteke introduced me to the shopkeeper as *'Ye humare saab hain'*.

That somehow, put me in a very awkward position. It was like the Raja had come to the market to see how his *praja* was doing. Which meant that I must behave like a king, like one who would set everything right for them by his visit.

Some shopkeepers would take that in their stride and start cribbing about the million problems they had, expecting me to wave a magic wand which normally meant offering them one better deal than what Ramteke was authorized to do. The only problem here was that even though I could take up this mantle of King, I didn't have a clue about what the Raja was supposed to do, because as I said, it was only his first day on the job! My desire was to learn from the shopkeeper as much as I could about his business, while his desire was to exploit *saab's* rare visit to the market. That put both of us in quite a dilemma, with me sitting in the shop like a dork not knowing what to do, or sipping the tea he would regret ordering later.

After completing a round of some small shops, a couple which were just six feet by four and the owner crouching in the center, Ramteke took me to few big stores which had godowns in the backyard and tens of people working all over the property.

'That was the retail sir,' he said, 'and this is the wholesale.'

'So wholesale means bigger shops,' I said, 'and retail means small outlets, right?'

'Sirrrr…mmmm,' it was like Ramteke wanted to say something but didn't know how to put it. 'Retail can be a big shop as well sir, but it sells only to consumers. Wholesale also sells to retail.' He put it in a way that doesn't make me lose face.

'Oh okayyyyyy, I get it,' I said, with an enlightened expression, as if the Einstein within me had just woken up, 'but tell me one thing Ramteke, when we already visit retail like we just did, why do they need to buy from wholesale?'

This time Ramteke couldn't hide his emotions. He looked at me as if he had just received the shock of his life, and he didn't even try to put it euphemistically, 'Sir,' he said, 'You are an MBA right?'

I nodded.

'Don't they teach you that?'

There it was – one year of hardcore preparations, two years of study, lakhs of rupees in fees, the big degree certificate and the framed photograph that hung in my parents' living room had just gone down the drain. So I was an MBA who couldn't tell the difference between retail and wholesale and my salesman couldn't digest the fact that this person was going to be his boss for a few months! The derisive look he gave me made me search for a hole I could bury my face in.

'They do,' I said, trying to do some damage control, 'there was a little confusion I was trying to address.'

'Sir, do we visit all the retail outlets?' His tone had now taken a patronizing tone.

'Maybe not?' I answered with apprehension.

'No one can visit all the outlets. This is what wholesale is for, to fill the gaps which we leave. And then there are some outlets which cannot buy a week's stock at one go. Not enough money. They are the ones for whom wholesale is a second resort.'

'But won't they be charged a higher rate?' I interjected, 'after all, wholesale will keep a margin for itself as well, won't it?'

'Yes, you are right. But they will trade it for comfort of supply,' he replied with a smile., 'Walk the markets sir, there is no one stop solution for anything. One question can have ten different answers. *Dheere dheere sab seekh jaoge.*'

That's how Ramteke Ji became my teacher. He had first taught me discipline, and was now teaching me sales. They are both closely related, as I would find out later, but couldn't comprehend that day. Some things no amount of education and degrees can instil, but runs in the veins with experience. I sat pillion on his Splendor, rode at a steady 50 kmph, walked the market the whole day. Some would welcome us with open arms, others would shoo us away from a distance. Some would sit with us and discourse on their business, others wouldn't have a minute to respond to a greeting. Some would have their orders ready for Ramteke, yet others wouldn't budge even after a zillion attempts at persuasion. By the time the day ended, I had visited some 25 outlets. Ramteke had orders from 12 of them, a business of approx. Rs 10,000, while I had a diary full of notes. As I walked back to my hotel room that night, Day One had taught me the third and most important lesson of my training – Patience.

NUMBERO UNO

Is that understood?

'The objective of your stint in Chattisgarh is to do your numbers,' said my boss, Regional Sales Manager for Central India. Although his name was Atul Singh Rana, people used to call him Tiger Rana, a nickname derived from the ferocity with which he would go after his targets. A man in his late thirties, he had been with IOC for nearly a decade, and had had tens' of boys like me parade before him during that period. He had a stout frame, a brisk walk and a sharp and commanding voice.

'A market is like a battlefield my friend', he continued, 'and in a battlefield there are no friends,' he concluded. The perhaps unintended paradox was not lost on me and I could barely prevent myself from laughing. He stood up, walked towards me, placed both his hands on my shoulders, and said, 'Do you know when an army man sits inside a tank marching towards his post, what the temperature inside the tank is?'

'N…no sir, I don't.' I replied, feeling the weight of his arms on my shoulders. I feared he might discharge me for fifteen rounds of the city grounds anytime soon.

'55 degrees Celsius,' he stated and paused, as if allowing me time to comprehend this inhuman feat. 'But the brave soldier doesn't complain. You know why, because he is in a battlefield. In the same way, be it rain or sun, winds or fire, you must neither complain nor come up with excuses when you fight your competition in the market. Do you understand me?'

'Yes sir. I do sir.' I was not quite sure whether to be inspired or intimidated.

'If you do your numbers,' he continued, calming himself down and settling back in his chair, as if transforming himself from a frontline Captain to the Army General, 'regardless of what you have done or how you have done it, we will consider you to have been trained. And if you do not do your numbers, regardless of anything or everything you might have done, we will consider you are not trained.'

He looked straight into my eyes, as if I was a criminal in his grasp and he had just completed the first round of interrogation. 'IS THAT UNDERSTOOD?'

Tiger Rana, it seemed, had given me thirty days to understand that statement, while I had not set any such deadline for myself. So when the first month of my training ended with an achievement of merely 69% in target numbers, I felt like a fish thrown out of water and left gasping to survive. Not knowing what else to do, I asked around and was led to a man they told me could be my savior – DKD.

Mr. Dayashankar Kumar Dayal, or DKD, as he was referred to was a civil engineer by profession. He had given up building bridges long ago and taken up something more suited to his talents – minting money from selling mint. In other words, he was the biggest distributor for IOC Foods Division for the state of Chattisgarh, catering to the triple markets of Raipur, Bhilai and Bilaspur.

It was difficult to figure out reasons for his success. Some said it was his honesty towards work, while an equal number put it down to his shrewdness. Some thought he was good at building relations, while others scorned his unyielding, stubborn ways. Some would attribute it to his generosity, others would brand him tight-fisted. Most people hated him yet loved him, despised him yet admired him.

The fact that he contributed more than 70% of IOC's business for the state single handedly, gave him more power over the market and clout in the head office than many would have liked. Many managers wanted to throw him out of the system, or at least reduce their dependence on him. But every time such a move was attempted, DKD would turn in better numbers. He was considered a necessary evil and left alone.

'*Maha Bekaar Aadmi*,' said DKD, handing over cups of tea to what he considered the decoration in his office, 'This is what I believe an MBA is today. Sir *lijiye* please.'

'*Pakki baat bhau*,' said Raju Seth, his trade partner from Jagdalpur, apparently in town on a business visit. 'My nephew, he had also gone to study this. And not even in Jagdalpur, I send him all the way to Nagpur. So high fees we pay, now he is back, and what does he know? He will teach me how to run a business? I said, *beta*, you won't learn business by reading a book. It takes experience to master the tricks of the trade, like we did, isn't it Dayal *saab*?'

'Sir, *kuch aur lenge*?' said DKD as he leaned towards me, in a tone that suggested flattery but was not, 'Raju Seth,' he said, making an introduction, 'Sir *hain*, from IOC. Chattisgarh is under his rule now.'

Raju Seth bent forward and joined his hands into a Namaste, while putting on a broad smile in a supposedly warm welcome to his land. 'I know Dayal *saab*,' he continued, 'we have met before, when he came to Jagdalpur. I am sorry sir I was really busy that day so couldn't spend much time with you. After that I left town for some urgent work. *Vaise bhi*, most of the business is now handled by Ramteke. I am just for namesake, to sign those bills maybe, he is the real owner, you know what I mean. I hope you faced no problem while you were there?'

'No, no, Raju Seth,' I replied, 'no problem at all. It has definitely been an enriching experience so far. Ramteke is a sincere and honest person, and very knowledgeable too, amazing control over his market. We are lucky to have people like him in our sales force, and you are lucky to have him in your market.'

'Couldn't agree more Sanjay ji, honesty is what's most important. God has given a lot to a small town man like me, may the remaining years too be lived in grace. Dayal *saab*, will take your leave now. It's nearing dusk, and I must get back home in time. My wishes to Bhabhi.'

DKD got up to bid adieu to Raju Seth while I sat back admiring the mini *darbar* he had set up in his premises. The room was a small 6X6 structure, with a wide table at one end behind which sat DKD, and spacious enough to allow not more than two chairs in the remaining area. A split AC placed right behind DKD soothed the nerves and cooled the temper while the call bell fixed just beneath the table ensured someone amongst his one hundred and eight strong workforce was always at his beck and call.

On one wall hung a large frame, with a garlanded picture of an old, bearded man, under which was written in bold black letters – Shri Shivshankar Kumar Dayal, which I assumed was of his late father, even though I wondered why 'Late' didn't precede the title. Just beside the frame was a wall-hung mini temple. It was an effective design I must say, because it ensured God doesn't occupy too much space in the already cramped office, and allowed the devotee to worship the deity while standing up, hence not consuming much of his time but also ensuring the prayers reach the Almighty's ears without fail.

Whilst I sat back admiring the ingenuity of DKD's office decor, I heard a voice call out, 'Sorry to leave you waiting sir.' It was DKD closing the door behind me, 'Raju Seth is a dear friend. You can say we started this business together, about ten years ago.'

'I could see that Dayal *saab*. Nice to witness the warmth between you,' I said with a smile.

'Friendship sir, that is what it is all about, isn't it? It's not just that your Facebook generation has friends. We too value it. Our friends may be fewer in number but they are rare, and we cherish them.'

DKD pressed the bell under his table.

'*Pakodi, ek* plate. *Chutney* sir?'

I hesitantly nodded.

'*Chutney ke saath*.' The aide sprinted off.

'To be honest sir, I am a little worried about him.'

'Who? Raju Seth? Why Dayal *saab*?'

DKD took a deep breath. 'Few years back sir,' he said, 'Raju Seth had a thriving business. Not just yours, but several companies used to trade with him. You can say he was one of the biggest businessmen in whole of south Chattisgarh. Then about three years ago, his two year old grandson died. It was an incurable ailment doctors say, some kind of cancer. I wouldn't know. He ran from pillar to post, to Nagpur, Mumbai, Delhi. I am not a doctor, but they say the boy slept one night and didn't wake up the next morning. Since then, he just stopped taking interest in his business. Shut trading with most of the companies, reduced in scale with others. Yours is one of the last few remaining, and even how that is managed you have yourself seen.'

'I understand your concern Dayal *saab*, I am sure everything will pan out just fine,' I said, without intending to be too patronizing or indifferent.

'Dayal *saab*,' I spoke up again after a few minutes, stuffing my face with the *pakodies*, 'I wish to discuss this month's business with you. Last month you know was a disaster. In your territory as well, we fell short of our targets by almost 30 per cent. We can't allow the same to happen this month again. This is season time you know, stakes are higher.'

'Business is down sir, you know that,' he replied, 'you think I am not worried? I am not a salaried person like you. The lesser I sell, the lesser I earn. I have a family to support.'

DKD ran an empire worth Rs. 30 crore in annual turnover, IOC being just one chunk of the huge pie. He had ten godowns spread across the state, along with a manufacturing unit of a local mint candy, which he had branded after a famous cricketer, and called it Sachinn mint. With two n's in the tail, no one could raise a trademark infringement claim against the product. Being cheap, sweet and Sachinn stamped, the mint was a runaway success in the glorious dust lands of Chattisgarh.

'I do understand Dayal *saab*, you have a family to support. We all have. And that is why I think we must take proactive action this time.'

'Sir, you don't understand, competition is getting tougher by the day. Yesterday itself I went to Aggrawal, that bastard is demanding 12% net, a bloody 2% extra. Where am I going to pay him from? By starving my son? By selling my daughter? And with all due respect sir, what is IOC doing about it? Nothing. Look at the petrol prices, the goddamn labor lives like kings now and we like beggars.'

Aggrawal was by far the largest wholesaler in the town of Raipur. And I can safely state that every month he would account for almost 10% of DKD's business with IOC. I must here also admit that if what DKD said was true, his demand for 12% profit margin on sale was by any standard exorbitant and unreasonable.

'That is bad, Dayal *saab.* This Aggrawal is holding us to ransom. We must teach him a lesson. But then, did he not buy anything last month? How is that possible? He also has to run his shop, doesn't he?'

'Sir, these scoundrels I tell you, they suck your blood until your last breath. I begged and begged and begged. Please buy IOC mint, please, please, please. After all, it's not the first time, is it? It's a ten year old relationship I said. Children demand it, would it look nice if you sent them away empty handed? How many rounds I took to his shop you don't know sir, and it was not just some salesman or any servant, I went myself, personally. But that bloody bugger, he didn't budge an inch. He said if you can't give me 2% extra, then please don't come to my shop. I said I can't, I don't have that budget. This is the best the company is giving me. Then he retorted, 'Fine then, is there anything else that the company is not giving you? Something cheaper maybe? What about Sachinn mint? What discount can you give on that?' I told him that is not what I have come to sell. It's either IOC mint or no mint at all.'

'Hmm,' I replied, 'so you refused to sell him anything?'

'Yes I did sir. I sure did. I said either IOC mint or no mint at all, you decide. And I walked out of his shop. I can fast unto death but not betray the company that has made me what I am, isn't it? But you know what happened sir? What that cheapskate scoundrel did? The next day one of my delivery boys visited his shop, you know, to deliver some other goods. Aggrawal asked him what discount is running on Sachinn, and that idiotic bastard told him 15%. Without even telling me, the next day he even dispatched the stocks, and placed this bill in my hands. I have decided to fire him anyhow. But sir, will that really solve the problem? We must find some solution, isn't it?'

'We definitely need to Dayal *saab*,' I replied, 'I know Aggrawal was being a pain even when we visited him last time. But I was wondering Dayal *saab*, in Jagdalpur last month, we did manage 90% of our targets. I toured all the markets with Ramteke and I saw no problem with our rates or competition.'

'Hah!' exclaimed DKD, with a snort, 'then why don't we do the whole state's numbers from Jagdalpur Sanjay sir, that would be the best solution, wouldn't it?'

I let the comment pass. There were a few moments of uncomfortable silence in the room, before he spoke up again.

'No offence sir, but you are new right now. Tell Rana sir what I told you, and he will understand. All these years, he has always blessed us.'

'I will look into it,' I replied, breaking eye contact. I believed the conversation was not proceeding towards a fruitful end.

'Don't take me wrong sir, but please understand our plight', he continued, 'when we stop monthly trading, everyone starts taking us for granted. Look at Aggrawal, since we didn't supply stocks to him last month, he hasn't even cleared his September bills till now. And it's not just he, nearly all of them do that. So much of my money is stuck in the market. You must help us by extending our credit limit sir.'

'You are already two months above your limit Dayal *saab*,' I stated firmly.

'You do trust us sir, don't you? I am just stating a solution. We have been together for ten years, you know your money is safe. But it might just help us get through these bad times. Rest is up to you sir, and your good sense. All I wish is to get our business back on track. That's all.'

***

A few days later Tiger Rana called me into his office. It was around the middle of the month and he wanted to take stock of the situation. It would be naïve to say he didn't already have a firm grip on it, which by all accounts, was grim. We were crawling at 20% of our targets, primarily because of the sluggishness in DKD's territories.

'He is asking for an additional 2% over and above his margins sir, because of which we have no progress in his territory,' I said.

'What about other territories?' he queried.

'They are all doing fine,' I replied, 'but as we know, DKD accounts for nearly 70% of the state's total sales. We can't even imagine reaching anywhere near our numbers with his markets performing badly.'

'Then give him his 2%, why don't you?' he reasoned.

'That is grossly unfair sir. Truth is he is promoting his own product, Sachinn mint. And he has conspired with the major wholesalers in his market, to demand extra discounts on IOC mint which he then wheedles from our pockets. Otherwise he sells them his own stock. I am sure it is just his trick. He will keep all that 2% himself, or maybe share a part of it. '

'A soldier can't make excuses my friend,' Tiger Rana roared, 'I am telling you, don't try to become an unnecessary hero, give him his 2%, you can say it is my order.'

'No sir I won't,' I shot back, 'this is blackmail, and we must not succumb to it at any cost.'

'Hmm,' he lit a cigarette as he leaned back in his chair, 'so what else are you going to do?'

'I have a plan of action sir,' I said, with a glint in my eye and earnestness in my voice. This is where I had envisioned transforming all my ideas of sales into action. 'The actual problem here is that the control of the market lies with DKD.

But at the same time, it is our sales force that goes to the markets on his behalf, isn't it? Look at the Jagdalpur market, where Ramteke has exceptional control. We need to make sure that it is our sales force that powers our sales and we are not caught in the machinations of DKD. I would run a productivity drive for his territory and incentivize our boys on their targets. Out of the 2% he demands, I only ask for half, just 1% of the budget. I would visit the markets myself, setup continuous monitoring systems. I am sure we will see results by month end.'

'Okay,' Tiger Rana chuckled. He too had a glint in his eye I couldn't help notice. 'I give you your 1%. Do whatever you want to do, but when the calendar clocks 30th, I want the numbers on my desk. Is that understood?'

***

I was a happy man. This is what I had fought with Baap for, isn't it? To be in FMCG sales. *It's not the only thing that I want to do, Raagini, but it's nearest to what I do best or what I love to do, and it's safe.* It was the time to prove myself, to Baap, to Sendu, to Tiger Rana, to Karan, to the world, to myself. And all I had with me were sixteen days – 15 to 30 November. Sixteen days, so short a time in the world. Sixteen days, and the hands of the clock had never run faster before.

I called all the men in my sales team and told them my plan. I discussed with Ramteke, my idol, the strategies I could follow. I made incentives for each one of them based on their targets, broken down into slabs of 80% and 100%, plus a bonus on over achievement. And from there on, I was on the road, walking the markets, literally. Raipur, Bhilai, Bilaspur, Korba, Raigarh, Ambikapur, Bastar, Kanker, Dhamtari, Jagdalpur, there was no town in the state I didn't visit. Travelling to all major markets myself, talking to the key retailers and wholesalers, dealing with all the Aggrawals I would have a face-off with. I was determined to not fall prey to the blackmail of DKD, and the only power I had in my hands was the strength of my team, the pull of my brand and the conviction of my heart.

Thirteen days went by swiftly. It was the dawn of 28th November. Temperatures had dipped to below five degrees Celsius. Some said it was one of the coldest winters they had seen in years. The streets were deserted, the trees swayed gently in the numbing breeze. Heaters, geysers and the makers of woollen garments were having a field day, businesses had shot up like never before. Small groups of people wearing mufflers and hats, coats and gloves would quietly pass by on the sidewalks, and small animals had settled down in their burrows, hibernating. But not me. I was walking briskly towards my office with head held high. From a 20% thirteen days ago, numbers were up to 70%, without paying an ounce extra to DKD. Several markets had been cracked, even Aggrawal, though only partly. I wanted to meet Tiger Rana.

'Good morning Sir, may I please come in?' I asked, gently knocking on the door.

'A very good morning Sanjay,' Tiger Rana replied, 'sure, please do come in. Have a seat. The chill doesn't seem to affect you, no caps or coats to fortify the walls?'

'Haha,' I chuckled, while seating myself on the chair opposite him., 'Nothing like that sir. It's just that I am actually from the hills so the cold doesn't really get in through these walls. Natural protection you see.'

'Good. Good,' he chuckled, 'we could always use tough men like you. Tell me, how are your numbers going?'

'Going great sir,' I replied, bubbling with enthusiasm, 'we have grown to 70% of the monthly targets. All markets have been performing well.'

'Hmm,' he replied, frowning, 'where do you think you would reach by the 30th?'

'I am confident we will touch 85% sir. From only a 69% last month, and all the growth we have seen is without budging an inch towards DKD's demands. In fact sir, he has been forced to place billing due to demands from the market. Ambikapur, Bilaspur, Raipur, Bhilai, Jagdalpur, all markets have done well.'

'Your 85% is not good enough Sanjay, do you realize that?'

'I know it's not 100% sir but we must look at the situation in hand and understand that…'

'Look at what Sanjay?' he interrupted, 'you know where Maharashtra stands today – 94%, MP-92%, even the laggard Andhra is doing better than you. What are you trying to make me understand?'

'Sir, what we have achieved is without heeding to any blackmail. The Raipur market has begun to find its feet outside of DKD's manipulations. We would need more time before it can fully recover. But the signs are positive, you can yourself see.'

'If we had paid him the 2%, we would have touched our 100% by now. Do you not see that?' his tone smelt of derision and anger. 'What did I tell you when we met the last time? I want the numbers on my desk by 30th. Show me my bloody numbers, where are they?'

I kept quiet. I had no further answers to his question. I couldn't say where I had gone wrong, but if Tiger Rana said so, I must have. The man had been awarded seven Outstanding appraisals in a row, rising up the ranks more swiftly than anyone else in the system. It was obvious he knew his do's and dont's better than I did.

'You don't know what kind of pressure I face from the head office,' he continued, 'you think I have the luxury of excuses? I can't tell my boss that the signs are positive, but we are yet to

TWENTY FOUR SEVEN

You can take leave from work,
but work will never take leave from you

'Didi! Didi, where are you?' Chintu was shouting at the top of his voice.

Raagini was sitting in her room, watching TV, surfing through the channels as Chintu's cries pierced the closed door.

'Didiiiiii, Papa is looking for you, where are you?' Chintu breezed through the house on his new skates, something he had recently learnt at a school camp and was proudly showing off to all the guests in the house.

'Here you are!' he exclaimed, pushing open the door. He rolled to her side and grabbed her hand.

'Have been looking all over for you, why didn't you reply? Come, Papa is looking for you,' he said, tugging at her hand.

Raagini shook his hand off. 'Leave me alone Chintu' she snapped 'What is the matter? Why are you shouting?'

'Papa is looking for you didi, come.'

'But why? What's so urgent that you are making such a racket?'

'He wants you to bring out some tea…few guests have come.'

'Chintu tell Papa I am not feeling well. I really don't feel like coming out. Get the maid to arrange for it na. Go, please tell her.' Suddenly her voice was loving and pleading.

'I can tell her that, but didi, Papa still wants you to come. Come na.' He took hold of her hand again.

'Why Chintu? Can't I just have some rest here?' The annoyance returned to her voice.

'Bishwas uncle has come, and Puneet bhaiya also. Papa wants you to come and meet them.'

The Bishwases and Malhotras were old family friends. Puneet's father Mr. Bishwas, and Raagini's father, Mr. Malhotra, were friends from college and had settled down in the same city. Raagini sent Chintu off with a message, 'Tell Papa I will be there soon.' She heaved herself out of bed and got ready. She knew Puneet had come to meet her and her dad wanted to see them together. She didn't want to be rude.

Fifteen minutes later, she came out wearing a yellow suit with a contrasting navy blue dupatta. She touched Mr. Bishwas' feet and sat on the sofa beside her father, avoiding eye contact with anyone. Even though she didn't look up, she knew everyone in the room exchanged glances waiting for her to speak. She didn't utter a word. Neither did she get up to offer refreshments to the guests, something her mother had specifically asked her to do. She didn't consider herself a showpiece that a prospective groom had come to admire and take home if he so wished. 'So, beta,' Puneet's father broke the awkward silence, 'how is work going?'

'Very well, uncle.'

'Nice nice,' Mr. Malhotra smiled broadly, 'even Puneet is doing great now. He is going to California, did he tell you?'

She gave a thin smile at both of them, acknowledging the information given to her. She didn't wish to be told the import of it, since she knew what it was. A few weeks from now she would be waking up late at night to have skype calls with him and indulge in pointless chatter. Her father would like that and she had to be a good daughter. Just like she was being right now.

'IOC is a good organization,' said Puneet, 'one of my friends also works there, Deepanshu Dutta, do you know him?'

She shook her head slightly. Puneet waited for her to say something. She knew she was being rude. She also knew Puneet was not a bad guy and she had no qualms about calling him a decent friend, someone she had known since childhood. If she had been asked to simply chat with him without any expectations she would have discussed Russia's foreign policy without batting an eyelid. But that was not the case and it bottled her up. She had wondered sometimes if she should tell her parents about it but she knew it wouldn't make a difference. She had already fought a battle to go for an MBA and delayed the inevitable by a couple of years. Anything more would not only disrupt harmony within the family but also destroy her father's age old friendship with dear Mr. Bishwas.

'Papa, can I go back now?' she was nudging her father half an hour later.

'Why? What is the problem? Stay back na. Why don't you and Puneet go for a walk?'

'Papa, I am really not feeling well,' she begged, 'please excuse me today, Please.'

She paid her regards to the guests, a formal greeting to Puneet and started walking back towards her room. She didn't want to be alone with him, she wouldn't know what to say. Chintu and his friends were playing in the verandah just outside her room. She called her pet dog and walked towards the terrace, where no one could see her, call her, reach her. She brushed the dust off one of the steps with her dupatta and sat down, stroking the dog mindlessly. Few minutes later, she took out her phone and dialed a number.

***

Sitting alone in my room in Raipur, I was pleasantly surprised to receive Raagini's call. It had been quite some time since we talked. One reason was that I had got busy with work, but the real reason was that I didn't know whether I should call her or not. I had last seen her at Chennai airport when she had come to drop me off. Since then I had longed to meet her, but all we had shared were a few random chats over the internet in between.

'Hello,' she said, as I picked up the call.

'Raagini, hi,' I concealed my apparent excitement, 'what a pleasant surprise. How are you?'

'I'm fine. Some people get their dream jobs and just forget their friends, isn't it?' she said teasingly.

'No, you know that's not true. Just got little busy with work, that's all.'

'How is it going,' she asked, and I could sense she had a broad smile on her face, 'I know you would do wonders in your new role.'

'Thank you Raagini,' I wanted to say a lot more than that. 'I am happy you called.'

'You know what Sanjay, Puneet has come to meet me,' she said after a brief pause.

'Puneet who?' I asked.

'Remember I told you, a family friend's son. His parents have also come. He is the one my parents want me to marry.'

'Then you should go and meet him, shouldn't you?' I replied curtly. I didn't want to be rude. I didn't. But I didn't want her to call me if she was anyway going to marry someone else, especially when that guy was sitting in her living room.

'Oh shut up Sanjay. Don't talk like Papa. You know I don't…,' she stopped midway, without completing her sentence.

'You don't what?' I prodded.

'I don't like him. I told you that, didn't I?'

'You told your parents?'

'No,' she replied tersely.

'Then go and tell them, and tell Puneet and his parents.' I wanted her to be honest with herself, and with me.

'Why did I even call you?' she said, sounding annoyed. 'Leave all this, it's a boring topic anyway. Remember that story you once mailed me? What was the title, Nametag or something, remember?'

'Of course I remember, Raagini. Did you read it?'

'Yes I did, Mr. Saklani. You do have a different style I must say. And you know what, I also sent it to a friend of mine, she works in a media agency in Mumbai. She has a friend, some kind of an artist, a director or a photographer or something. Sagar Shah, if I am not wrong. He was looking for an English writer. She sent him your story. He liked it and he says he wants to meet you. Tell me that's not the gift you always wanted! And now you will thank Raagini, won't you? Call him up. I will send you the number. If you come next week, I might also be there. Some office work. Will you take me to dinner Mr. Bigshot?'

***

Sagar Shah had a website by his name, which read www.sagarshah.com. More than the website itself, I was impressed by the fact that in this world of web clutter he could have a domain available to his name. The next thing I did of course was to search for www.sanjaysaklani.com, not because the narcissist in me thought that God might have made me a celebrity overnight but purely because I imagined Saklani was a much more uncommon name than Shah, and hence should have been more readily available. It was, and I was tempted to register it. If only I had something to write in.

Sagar Shah did, he was an acclaimed theatre person, a writer, photographer, director. Not a person with much commercial success yet, but whose last production had earned critical acclaim. He was recognised as one of the most talented and promising names in the field. There was a quote on the home page of his website, which said, 'Tests show a bumblebee can't fly in relation to its wing span, but the bumblebee doesn't know this, and it flies anyway'. I thought I was the bumblebee, the only difference being that even before leaping in the air I had already determined the flying capacity of my wing span.

Sagar Shah said he would be available only on the next Friday evening, which was a good thing. I could stay back over the weekend and meet Raagini. But the bad thing was that I would have to apply for leave to Tiger Rana. The Tiger though did not seem to be in a mood to hunt that day and let the prey go, although with a caveat: you can take leave from work, soldier, but remember, work will never take leave from you!

There are very few days which we remember as being truly happy in our lives, and that was one such day. I was excited. I was going to meet a person to be in whose shoes I would have given up the world. And I was not going there for an autograph or get a a photograph to frame and put in the living room, I was going there because he had asked for me, because he wanted to meet me for something that was mine; his instinct had acknowledged and appreciated it. And this appreciation was not for something I had done to please the society around me, to gain someone's favor or earn an A in someone's grade sheet, but it was something that had come right from the core of my heart and my soul. And knowing this alone was God's greatest gift to me, irrespective of what might happen later…

'Sanjay hi, this is Sagar,' he said, as we seated ourselves in one of the bustling coffee shops in the suburbs of Mumbai. A man of his word, he was there at 9 pm sharp. He didn't seem old, maybe somewhere in his mid thirties with a youthful face, a soft spoken manner, casual dress sense and light hearted banter. A man completely at home in the milieu. My thoughts raced back to the image of Tiger Rana sitting in his chair blowing smoke rings into the air and pounding his fist on the table. I had respect for the sincerity demanded by Tiger Rana, but I was instantly gripped by the insouciance of Sagar Shah.

'Hello sir, it's really an honor and a pleasure to meet you,' I replied, meaning every word of it.

'Don't call me sir Sanjay, Sagar is fine,' he said, 'I read your story, Nametag, right, have you brought a copy or synopsis of it?'

I was carrying a hard copy of Nametag and also of two other stories I had written.

'Yes right, give me that,' he said, holding the folder in his hands, 'you know what is good about this story?'

'What Sagar?' I enquired innocently.

'That it comes from the heart,' he replied, 'it is not perfect, in no way is it perfect, in fact it is far from what a well-constructed short story should be. There is no clear premise, the female character has not been defined completely, the conflict does not create, or resolve itself clearly. There are a lot of loopholes. Your basic concept of a love story is a topic which has been handled several times before. Yet, it is different from a lot of stuff that I keep reading nowadays. Because it comes from the heart, it's not force cooked, and that is what makes it different.'

'Thank you, Sagar,' I was not sure whether I was being praised or mocked, but it sure sounded like encouragement.

'No, not yet. Look, I want you to convert this short story into a script, for a play. Do you understand me? I find your concept appealing. I can visualize it into a grand production. But you will have to write it, and only you can write it, because you are the one who has conceived of it. But you will have to put your head and heart into it.'

I was overwhelmed, a chance to stage my play! That would be grand. But at the same time I was worried. I had never written a script before. I didn't even know where to begin.

'That sounds great Sagar, really, thanks. But I don't quite know how to write a script. I have never written a script before. Just some stories like this here and there. How would I go would about it?'

'The most important thing Sanjay is to understand the premise of your whole thought,' he continued, gesturing animatedly, 'you should know what you are trying to communicate. At what emotion does it begin and with what emotion does it end. That is why I would have liked it if you had brought a synopsis with you. Here, craft it right now. Draw a flow diagram for the whole concept. The inception and the culmination and the interlinked emotions.'

To be honest, I didn't really understand a word of what he was saying. I tried to scribble a few words but couldn't manage anything.

'But how can I find a connection between these emotions?' I asked, looking to find my feet in the discussion. This was free tuitions to great scriptwriting, I didn't want to be caught napping.

'See, if you tell a girl that you love her, and she replies that she loves you too, would there ever be a story?'

'No,' I replied, 'it would be end of the story.'

'Exactly,' he replied, 'but now, if she can't love you back, or you both love each other but something doesn't allow you to be together, then there is conflict, there is intensity and that leads to drama. Now there are seeds of it in your story, but if you understand where it is coming from, the root of who your characters are, why they can't get what they want, you will be able to flesh it out better in your script.'

There was an Aha moment in my eyes. I thought I understood a part of what he was trying to say.

'I can't really teach you how to write a script, and it can't come from what you have already seen in other books or movies. Your characters must be unique in their own way, and genuine. If you get that right and put both your head and heart into it, it will start coming intuitively to you. Do you understand me?'

My cell phone lying on the table started ringing. It was Tiger Rana on the line. I didn't want to pick it up, I let it ring and put the device on silent mode. Two minutes later, it rang again.

'Just pick it up,' said Sagar, 'see what it is..'

'Hello, yes sir, Good evening,' I said.

'Evening Sanjay, where are you?'

'I am out of town sir, I had taken leave.'

'Yes right, I know,' he said, 'listen, we have a region-wise presentation to the National Sales Manager on Monday. Past performance, competition, projections everything has to be covered. I need you to make it tonight and send it to me by tomorrow afternoon. All right?'

'But sir,' I replied, 'I am occupied with some personal work. I really don't think I will have the time to prepare it by tomorrow afternoon. I'll come back on Monday and do it. Or maybe on Sunday?'

'Come on Sanjay, don't be a sissy boy. It's important and urgent, I want it by tomorrow morning in my mailbox, is that understood?' he said, as he cut the line.

My face fell.

'I am really sorry Sagar,' I apologized, 'let's continue.'

'Who was it?' he asked.

'That was my boss, I actually work in Raipur, I'd come down for the weekend.'

'Ok,' he nodded. 'But, why do you live in Raipur? You should live here, then we can also interact more often.'

I wish it were that simple!

'Actually,' I said, I have a job there so I live there.'

'You must be looking for something in Mumbai, right?'

'I guess so,' I nodded, though I was not sure if it was just *something* I was looking for. I had a good, plush job in Raipur. I didn't know whether I would want to replace it with *something* to come over to Mumbai.

I could see Sagar was dialing a number.

'Hi,' he was saying, 'there is a friend of mine. He is a writer, you know plays, theatre etc. he wants to come to Mumbai but he also wants to keep some job here.'

'In what field would you want to take up the job,' he asked me, putting the call on hold.

'Sales…aaa…or marketing maybe,' I replied, hesitantly.

'Sales or marketing,' he says, 'see if you find one and let me know, all right, great, thanks.'

He hung up.

It was the first time in my life someone had called me a writer. It made me feel proud, but at the same time insecure. Is he going to drag me down here to some run-of-the-mill job? I don't know how he runs his household but I would need a decent pay check if I have to survive in Mumbai, and also plan for the future, I thought to myself.

'You know where I used to work during my initial days?' he chuckled.

'Where?' I asked, curious.

'As a junior accountant in one of the law firms town side. I am a commerce graduate. But the good thing was it was a 9 to 5 job, so I used to get a lot of spare time after work. You seem to be working twenty four seven.'

A slight smile, which spoke of helplessness and acceptance flitted across my face. Did he not worry about planning for the future?

'It must have been quite a challenge, isn't it?'

'Monetarily you mean?' he said, 'It was, of course, I even got married quite early, I was in love. But we got by. It pretty much comes down to a simple choice Sanjay, what kind of compromise you want to live your life with, internal or external. Most people choose the former, I am not saying they are right or wrong. In my case, I had no other option. I had to choose the latter.'

He paused for a long moment, looked me in the eye and said,

'I look forward to seeing how you write this Sanjay. Don't rush yourself, Have something ready, a first draft, maybe by January or February. Keep in touch and share your progress with me. But don't send me anything until you have written and are satisfied with your first draft. Remember, put your head and heart into it. Good luck!'

The clock was ticking away the seconds dutifully. It knew exactly what to do and when. At one moment I wished I had its clarity, but at the next I decried its predictability. It was pitch dark as I walked back home that night. This is a great opportunity, I was saying to myself. And I must make the most of it. No matter what happens, from tomorrow onwards, every day I am going to give two hours to my script.

The next day I sat down with my presentation. It was a comprehensive report, and I knew it would take time, so I wanted to get it over and done with as soon as possible and dispatch it to Tiger Rana. He had already called twice since morning. I finally finished it by evening and hopped on the train to go to the beautiful Marine Drive, to meet Raagini. I never thought I would see her again. From the moment I left her at the airport in Chennai, I had prayed to God to give me one more day, when I could be with her again. And today, that day had come.

The Queen's Necklace was glowing in all its glory, bedecking the ravishing curves of the Mumbai skyline. The tide was high, and the waves lashed its carved contours. It seemed as if the city opened its arms wide to embrace the winds that blew from the far shores, welcoming every one that came to lie in its lap, offering its unconditional love. I had bought two tickets for a production running to a full house at the NCPA theatre. It had been quite a hit in the recent past, especially acclaimed for the sterling performance by the lead actress, a village girl whom the protagonist falls in love with, and who wears a backless choli throughout her performance. Raagini had expressed a desire to watch the play since the day it had been released. It was the perfect arrangement for me. Not only did I have an opportunity to fulfil one of Raagini's long awaited wishes, I also got to watch a quality production after ages. I hoped it would provide some inspiration for one of my own some day. The added attraction being, of course the backless choli!

'You really liked the actress, didn't you?' she asked as we stepped out after the play.

'She was good, played the role well,' I replied nonchalantly, ignoring the insinuation.

'Good is it? For the whole play you remained glued to her, why don't you go ahead and marry her.'

'I am thinking about it,' I said, again without batting an eyelid.

'Great,' she said, 'good for you. You know what, even I am thinking about Puneet.' She said the words, but I could tell she was faking it.

We had walked into a restaurant overlooking the sea, which actually lived up to its name. It had jazz music and served pizzas. But the music was so loud it meant paying cash to get in and then be punished for doing so. You couldn't hear each other sitting ear to ear. I would have preferred music, drinks, food and a conversation, especially when it was with someone I didn't get to converse with too often.

'He and his family came home for Diwali, did I tell you?' she continued, choosing a seat with a sea facing view.

'Yes, you did,' I replied.

'And did I also tell you I didn't feel like meeting him or talking to him?'

'Something like that, yes.' My reply was brusque, even dismissive.

'I don't want to hurt my parents Sanjay,' she said, with a forlorn look on her face, 'I don't know what to do.'

'You should do what your heart tells you to do. Listen to it,' I replied. I wanted her to believe in what she was doing and act upon it.

'Do you listen to yours?' she asked, looking into my eyes.

'I do,' I said, 'I do listen to my heart.'

'Then I have a question for you, how did it go with Sagar?'

'It went well, in fact, not just well, it went great, he said he liked my story, and he said he wants me to convert it into a screenplay. It was wonderful. It was… it was overwhelming.'

'So, what did you write today?'

'Today?'

'Yes,' she emphasized, '*today*. You are excited about it. This is your calling card you say. This is what your heart tells you to do. Yesterday, you got some direction, right? You had a full day today to pursue the path that is your dream, what did you do about it today?'

'I will Raagini, I sure will. But today I had to work on one presentation, it's on Monday, and my boss wanted me to finish it by today itself. I have finished it now, and sent it to him, so after going back and all day tomorrow, that is what I am going to do.'

My phone was ringing again. It was Tiger Rana on the line. I reached for it sheepishly. I could see she was glaring at it.

'Sir, good evening,' I said.

'Evening Sanjay, I saw your presentation.'

'Actually sir, I am in midst of something,' I replied hesitantly, 'can we please talk tomorrow?'

'Yeah sure, my friend. I will only take two minutes. Listen, I have seen it, there are a few changes I have marked in red. Make them tonight and send back positively, all right? And tomorrow, come to office in the evening, we will have an internal review. Enjoy your evening, cya.'

He cut the line. I switched off the phone and put it in my pocket. I wanted to spend the next day with Raagini. Was asking for two evenings being greedy? I didn't know when I was going to see her next, if ever. She was looking at me expectantly.

'What?' she said, as if she'd noticed the mournful look on my face.

'I have to work on the presentation tonight as well. And I have to go back tomorrow afternoon, have a meeting with boss in the evening.'

We both stayed quiet for some time after that, eating our pizzas by the bay. I wanted her to ask me to stay back for her for one more day and I would have. She wanted me to ask myself to stay back for one more day and work on my dream. Finally, she broke the silence.

'You know I read this somewhere,' she said, 'if you wait to become a writer, you are a waiter.'

'This is a new job Raagini,' I said, thinking hard, not really knowing what to say, 'it is not yet a year since I joined here. I should first settle down. There are several things to learn, people don't know me right now. I am just an employee code. To become a name, I have to perform. I can't make excuses even if it is 9 pm on the Saturday evening and I am with…'

I didn't finish the sentence. She didn't ask me to.

'Do you think your boss, what's his name, some Tiger, is he settled?'

'I think so. And he has a reputation. People know him in the organization. Nobody knows me right now.'

'Is he not working 9 pm on a Saturday night?'

He was. I didn't answer her question.

'Do you think Baap has a reputation?'

'He does,' I replied, 'tremendous!' I wondered where she was going with this.

'Do you know he has been asked to leave?'

'What?' I shot back in surprise. I had a ready to drop dead look on my face. Since I had moved to Chattisgarh, I had not been in touch with the happenings at SGD. Baap asked to leave? How could that be possible? He was one of the backbones of the company. He was the one who set up the whole SGD for heaven's sake!

'What are you saying, Raagini?' I asked incredulously. 'He has been asked to leave? What do you mean?'

'There has been an issue in one of SGD's businesses. The business head wanted to disinvest, but Baap didn't want to. It was a good financial decision, but involved a significant amount of layoffs. He was against that. The issue went to the Chairman and grew into a tussle. First he was stripped of the controls of this business, and then three more. He is left with just the printing unit now, nothing more than a ceremonial head. He has not been asked to leave in a literal sense of course, but after all this, a person of his stature, you wouldn't expect him to stay back, would you?'

'And what is happening now?' I asked.

'This might be his last month in the company. And you know something, after 36 years of service, he is not being given an official farewell.'

This was too heavy a news for me to digest. I remembered the days a few months ago when I was in Chennai, the way he walked, talked, conducted himself. The way all of us used to idolize him. The way the whole organization used to idolize him. The way he had pushed me to explore myself, stretch myself. And then, within a span of a few months?

'He spent thirty six years building a reputation Sanjay, didn't he? And what happened? One decision where he stood his ground and not buckle under pressure, refusing to say what his boss wanted to hear, ...pffft all gone! I don't know what his priorities in life were, but you know yours, if they really are your priorities, that is. You don't know how lucky you are to know what you want. Make that count while you can. Prioritize. Otherwise, there will always be something more important to do.'

She said she wanted to visit the Gateway of India, to wave at the boats and ships bobbing in the sea or lounging in the harbour. As we walked towards one of its imposing pillars, we were approached by a young photographer. He flashed an album of over-smiling, 'happiest moment of their lives' couples and began regurgitating his sales pitch. 'For your lovely future sir, for the living room mam, a memoir of the Gateway sir, bound in the camera here binds the love for a lifetime mam.'

'No thank you,' I said, trying to shoo him away, 'we are also not together. We are friends, so you can leave.'

'For your lovely friendship sir, for the albums mam, a memoir of the Gateway sir, bound in the camera here binds the friendship for a lifetime mam.'

The photographer was a persuasive and persistent salesman. I thought I could learn a trick or two from him.

'What is the harm Sanjay?' she said, 'Let's get one clicked na.' She held my arm and took me to the front of the Gateway, checked her dress and her hair, and posed like a heroine. I stood there beside her while she clutched on to my arm. '*Bhaiya, acchi wali kheechna*,' she shouted at the top of her voice.

The photographer gave us two instantly developed pictures. Her round cheeks were glowing bright with her blithe smile and luscious lips. The wind from the sea was playing with her hair, willing them to flutter about her face. Her eyes were twinkling with the mischief of a kid who'd been gifted her favourite toy on her birthday. She held on to my arm as we walked around the Gateway, seating ourselves behind the edifice, facing the sea. The wind blew on our faces, our legs dangled randomly below the parapet, our bodies connected to each other, providing a comfortable warmth in the chilly evening.

'May I ask you a question Sanjay?'

'Anything Raagini,' I replied.

'When do you plan to marry?'

I was caught completely off guard. My parents had not asked me this question yet, so I could honestly say that I had never even thought about it, not even once. And now in a flash of a second, a girl I was crazy about, had put it right in front of my face. I came up with an honest, unrehearsed response.

'I don't know Raagini… I haven't thought about it yet.'

'Hmm,' she replied, and went quiet, staring into the vast ocean, as if she was looking for a refuge within it. We sat there for a few minutes, nothing but silence between our words, a battle lurking between our thoughts. A battle nobody wanted to wage and nobody desired to win. And yet it ensued, and we fought, blindfolded, with our hands tied behind our backs, while the rolling waves looked on like mute spectators. I turned to look at her. Her eyes were dark, as if a storm was brewing beneath the surface, yet hidden, concealed for now. Unanswered questions and unquestioned answers. A few seconds later, I put my hand around her, leaned forward, looked into her eyes for a long moment, and kissed her.

THE CHITRAKOOT FALLS

This is what I want to live for, or die for

The next day was a Sunday. The first twenty four hours post my resolve had slipped away, without a word put on paper. Prioritize, she had said. I flew back to Raipur but didn't go to office that day. I made the changes as desired and mailed them back to Tiger Rana. I told him I was occupied and wouldn't be able to make it to office on Sunday, but would come for the review on Monday. I sat down for the rest of the day, switched off my phone and started to write my script.

The review went just fine. The NSM was not so happy that he jumped up and kissed me, but he seemed not too disappointed either. 'Good job', he said, looking at my previous month's achievement, 'but I want more.' I had no idea what he meant by *more*. After the lights went off and the cameras rolled out, Tiger Rana summoned me to his office.

'Why didn't you come to office yesterday?' he asked, skipping the pleasantries.

'I was busy with some personal chores sir, as I had already informed you,' I replied.

'Do you think Nishant is a fool that he came all the way from Nagpur? Do you think Sunil is an idiot that he came from Bhopal? Do you think I am a fool that I preferred to go to office on a Sunday evening to look at your presentations instead of spending time with my family? You were the local guy, the review was in your office, your territory, and you are the one person who is missing. Do you think we are all fools?'

'No sir, I don't think so. I am just saying I had some urgent work that I couldn't leave midway.'

'Either you are dead or you show up, that is the rule. Do you understand?' he thundered, 'Why was your phone switched off?'

'It was switched off because I didn't want to be disturbed. What about some work life balance sir? It was a Sunday, and I had already done my work, so I thought...'

'Don't think,' he reprimanded, 'you disobeyed a direct order, Sanjay. And at so young an age you talk of work life balance? You are at the beginning of your career. Don't give me weekdays and weekends and work life and personal life and all that. At this point you should be willing to work your ass off, to put your nose to the grindstone, to run the last lap even if that is your last breath. This is a competitive world, with your attitude you will never be able to climb the ladder, you'll get lost, you will be like an insignificant dot in the crowd.' He paused for a moment, and then in a gentler voice said, 'Tell me one thing, what is your goal?'

'Goal sir, meaning?' I asked, perplexed.

'Like your objective in life? Isn't it to become a CEO of some big firm? Some big, famous organization with Sanjay Saklani its Chief Executive Officer, isn't it? It's not a 100m sprint, it's a marathon. We are all long distance runners, with one eye on the goal.'

'Actually sir,' I replied tentatively, 'my goal is not to become a CEO of some big firm.'

'It is not?' he blurted out, stupefied. 'Then what?'

'Do good, meaningful work that satisfies me,' I said, putting together my thoughts carefully, 'be good to the people around me, have a good life, be happy. Follow my heart, my passion. If doing that makes me some CEO, great, but becoming a CEO is not what I am living for.'

'Those words look good as a punch line Sanjay,' he smiled, 'to be quoted in articles, to inspire people in movies or sell cola in advertising, not in real life.' I remained silent. He spoke up again.

'You are young, unmarried, no liabilities, so you can afford to talk like that. You have not yet seen the cruel hand of fate. You live in your cocoon, in a make believe world, where mommy washes the diapers and daddy cleans the pot. You know what I mean? Once you grow up, you are the one who needs to get your hands dirty. To survive. It's not live and let live anymore; it's either live, or die. You think only you have passions? Only you want to follow your heart? When I was young, I wanted to be in the army. I applied for NDA, SSB, CDS, couldn't make it, was rejected at different stages every time. I had to make a living. My family needed me to help make both ends meet. I applied for a job and joined sales. I too had a dream, but I wasn't a daydreamer like you. I was practical. People like you would say one should find work where one has passion, but it doesn't work that way. It's actually the other way round. If you want to be happy, you should find passion in your work, in your job, like I have done. Then you will not whine about work life balance,' he said, the disdain returning to his voice.

'Do you understand me?' he said, thumping the table for extra impact. 'I don't want this to be repeated ever again.'

I wondered how Vishwant or Sagar Shah would have countered his argument, if at all they bothered to. I wished they were there with me that day to give me an answer. 'Yes sir,' I said, giving him a salute, 'I understand,' and walked away.

***

The whole world was celebrating New Year, we had entered 2010. Raju Seth had been unable to clear his dues, and I was getting worried. I wanted to go to Jagdalpur, talk to Ramteke, but I wanted to do that unofficially. The opportunity presented itself on 14th January, the festival of Makar Sankranti. Ramteke told me how another north Indian sales manager like me once showed him about how they would celebrate Lohri in Delhi. Ramteke liked it so much that he combined both the festivals to create a unique celebration of his own. He insisted I had to come. I packed my bags and headed south.

The roar of the surging waterfall was deafening. Exploding through the rocks and plunging down a hundred feet or more, the mighty cascades declared their authority over the land. As if Mother Nature had devised these ingenious ways to show man who was the more powerful and the havoc she would cause should he dare to violate her. I stood there in complete silence, awestruck in the presence of such magnificence. It was the largest, the tallest, the broadest and the strongest waterfall I had ever seen – the Chitrakoot Falls, known as the Niagara Falls of India for its size and span, formed on the Indravati river. Chitrakoot was about 50 kms west of the town of Jagdalpur, en-route to Dantewada. From the sacred land of Hindu pilgrimage in the past it was now a region torn between strife, struggle and blood in the present.

'These falls are usually the place for naxal meetings sir,' Ramteke was saying, 'today the water flow is less, during monsoons, the roar can be heard as far as Dantewada.'

'Why don't the Naxals mend their ways Ramteke? What will come out of such guerilla warfare?' I asked curiously, like the student I usually became in his presence.

'They are revolutionaries in their own country sir. They didn't pick up the weapon out of choice, let me tell you. This is a beautiful piece of land; nature has been kind, it was known to be the abode of Lord Rama in the past. But this is not a rich piece of land. It's a daily struggle for food, water, clothing. When a man feels he hasn't got his due from society, he rebels.'

Ramteke's village was a small .township called Geedum, about fifteen kms from the town of Dantewada. His family had made arrangements for a small get together. Wood was collected from the nearby jungle and a huge bonfire had been constructed to celebrate in the evening. Apart from his family, Raju Seth, two more friends and myself were the only mentions in the guest list. I wondered if the village folk would wear some special tribal attire which I could capture in my camera and show off to my friends. But to my surprise and some disappointment, they wore ordinary normal clothes like ordinary normal people. What did stand out was the interior of their homes, replete with intricate hand-made artefacts, drawing their lineage to the unique Bastar handicraft art, called the *Dhokar.* Even though I was amongst friends, I was a little nervous. This was the heartland of the Naxalites and a non-touring territory according to IOC guidelines. No one would take responsibility if something happened to me that night. I wondered how Ramteke and his family happened to live there all these years, with a constant fear of bloodshed and death looming over their heads.

'Why do you continue to live here Ramteke?' I asked him, 'shouldn't you move somewhere closer to Jagdalpur or Bastar, a safer area?'

'Why should we sir? This is our home,' he replied defiantly. I thought he was unable to gauge the undertones in my suggestion.

'I know it is, but it is a dangerous area, don't you fear someday something might happen to you or your family?'

'It can sir, it sure can. But those who run are cowards. This is our land, we have lived here since generations. We can't abandon that simply because some misguided youth in the recent past have started thinking otherwise.'

'I think you are being an unnecessary hero Ramteke, putting your family's life in danger like this,' I remarked derisively.

'Sir, I appreciate your concern. You say so because you fear, you are new to this region. Everyone who is new has this fear. I was born here, grew up amongst these fields and the jungles, I belong to this place. I have seen people close to me joining the naxals or recruiting in the ranks of the CRPF. I have seen them die on both sides. We are a part of this battle, our lives are. I don't have that fear. A man cannot live his life in fear, sir. If he does, he is not living, he might be breathing all right, but he is dead from inside. Please, I want you to meet someone.'

He went inside the house and brought with him a handsome young man, possibly around twenty years old.

'Meet Sanjay sir,' he said, making the introductions, 'he is our boss in IOC. And Sir, this is Mahesh, my eldest son. He has joined the CRPF.'

I could see the pride in Ramteke's eyes. And justifiably so, for his son was a jewel to him. And yet he had allowed him to join the Central Reserve Police Force, a para military outfit. To send your beloved child into the jaws of the naxalite revolution was something I couldn't understand. Hundreds of jawans had lost their lives in the strife here in the last few years.

'Welcome to Dantewada Sanjay ji', his son was saying, 'have you come here for the first time?'

'Yes, first time', I nodded. 'I am sorry Mahesh, but I have to ask you this. Why did you join the CRPF? It is dangerous to live here even as a civilian, but as a CRPF jawan, it's a minefield. You can get killed any day.'

The boy gave me a frank innocent smile. 'Did you stop by the Chitrakoot Falls on your way here, Sanjay ji?' he asked.

'Yes I did,' I replied, 'it's a breathtaking , mesmerizing place.'

'Did you see any tourists in that place?'

'Not many Mahesh. Maybe around two or three. Why?'

'Till few years ago, when this revolution had not begun, the Chitrakoot Falls used to be throbbing with tourists. It is the largest waterfall in the country. People used to drive down from far to watch the falls. These hills, these caves, we live in a beautiful part of the country Sanjay Ji. But now, no one comes here, we have become a forgotten land, a lost tribe in our own home. It's as if Chitrakoot and Dantewada no longer exist on the map of the country. I want to bring back peace Sanjay Ji, to our homes, to our villages, to our lives. I am not saying I alone can change everything, but one man with courage is an army, isn't it? This is my dream, a new Dantewada, the Kashmir of Chattisgarh, Dantewada, the land of Lord Rama, Dantewada, a thriving tourist destination, a pilgrimage centre, a place where there is no fear, but only joy and happiness. And this is what I want to live for, or die for.'

I was impressed with the boy. There was passion, faith and zeal in his speech, his eyes. Ramteke stood beside us, smiling from ear to ear.

'Do you have a dream Sanjay sir?' he asked, breaking into the conversation, 'you will understand this if you have one.'

'Yes' I replied earnestly, 'I do.' I wanted to show them I was not just a programmed robot they might be taking me for.

'What is it, if I may ask?'

'I want to write a script and stage my own theatre production,' I said. This was the first time I had given words to it.

'Is it?' Ramteke was impressed, 'I didn't know you wrote or did theatre, sir! We have an artist amongst us! What is the script all about?'

'I am yet to write it Ramteke,' I said sheepishly, 'it's in the form of a story right now. I have to put it down.' After that one day, I had not had the time to write any more.

'Okay great,' he replied enthusiastically, 'when do you plan to write it and stage it? We will be one of your first fans!'

'Soon, Ramteke, I hope very soon. This job has kept me so busy for some time now, but once I get time, I will write.'

Ramteke stood quietly for a minute. 'Sir, let me tell you a story, of a man who wanted to swim,' he said. 'There were no ponds or lakes in the town where he lived so he had to move to a city where there was a swimming pool. He found out that if he had to live in the city, he had to pay rent. To pay rent, he took up a job. He worked for one full month and earned a salary. Using that money, he took a membership of a swimming pool and went there to swim.'

'I understand what you are saying Ramteke, but this man of yours had time to go swim after his job. I don't.'

'Why did the man go to the city in the first place, sir? Did he go there to do the job he took up? No, he went there to swim. His job was a means to it, not the end. I see several people, many of them in IOC just like you, who have come and worked with me. They also, like you, had several dreams. When we sat down after a hard day's work in the market, they would tell me all about it. People talk about their innermost feelings and desires after two pegs, don't they? And what do I see the next day when the hangover wears off? They have forgotten everything. They go back to their jobs, day after day, month after month, year after year. After some time, it really becomes all about the money. They forget what they had told me that night. They forget they had come to the city to swim.'

What Ramteke said made perfect sense. What Mahesh had said also made perfect sense. I could now understand why they had no fear or why Sagar Shah didn't worry about planning for his future.

The bonfire had been lit and everyone had gathered around it. Raju Seth was sitting on a charpoy kept nearby, as he was not feeling well. We walked around the fire, murmuring certain prayers Ramteke's family had advised me to. They offered us delicious home-made sweet and savoury snacks to munch while sitting beside the fire. While the prayers were being said, someone would keep rearranging the firewood so that the flames would keep burning brightly and strongly into the sky. After some time, I beckoned Ramteke to an isolated corner to have a chat.

'Ramteke, you remember the credit billing of November? When can we pay back that money? Soon the company will start charging interest, or might even put a block on the transactions.'

'I am sorry to say this sir but I think that was not a very smart step to take,' he replied. 'You know the potential of our town, and the current financial situation of Raju Seth. We can't make a man eat more than he can digest, can we? All he will do is vomit. More than half the stock you shipped is still lying in the godowns. Part of it we did sell in the market, but that was just pushed in by force. It hasn't even moved off the retailers' shelves yet, and hence they have not completed their payments.'

'Can we at least get some remittance by next week?' I asked in desperation.

'We can get some, maybe five. I talked to Raju Seth last week. He has not been keeping well these days. He said he would try and arrange for some funds from the other business.'

Even five lakhs wouldn't resolve the issue completely, but it would be a start, I said to myself. I was worried we might have to close his account, and send insurers down to his shop. On my recommendation, Ramteke was being considered for a promotion in the next financial year, and a blocked customer going to the insurer's desk would have hampered his chances considerably.

'Sanjay sir,' a voice called out from behind. Raju Seth was waving at me. 'You are our chief guest for tonight sir. What are you doing standing in an isolation away from us? Come, have a seat. Mahesh, we should have some entertainment, shouldn't we? Why don't you sing us a song?'

Mahesh went inside the house and brought out his mouth organ. He had bought it recently from Jagdalpur, and had mastered few tunes on it. He put it to his mouth as the audience fell silent in attention and anticipation. They told me he played one of the folk songs of the region whose title was 'Dantewada, the pride of Chattisgarh'. I didn't know the words and I didn't understand the local dialect, so I couldn't understand what the lyrics would have meant. But I could see him lost in his instrument and the music he played, the village folk cheering him on humming the song with him. Whatever those words might have tried to capture, I think immersed in the music, I got the message. O traveller, where you have pride, where you have a dream, there it is where lies your heart, there it is where lies your passion, binding souls together into one, not by caste, income or education, but by a purpose that knows no fear, but by a purpose thou can live for and die for, where you belong. And that is how, my man, you become great.

CHAOS

What option do I have anyway?

Like people and their emotions, seasons too come and go. They delude us with the promise of a future and then leave us bereft, yet with perpetual hope.

It was the time for winter to sneak out of our homes and leap into another part of the world. The vacations were over. Squirrels and rabbits lounging in their burrows would soon come scurrying out into the gardens; trees would lift up their drooping branches and prepare for another round of flowering. Children would prepare for their examinations, some with apprehension, others with excitement, happy to see the culmination of the whole year's efforts. Yes, the month of March was upon us, and I too had an examination to appear for. The year end was the biggest season of sales in our business. It accounted for nearly thirty percent of annual sales and this was the time to give it all. Especially because the year on the whole had not been great and this was an opportunity to make amends. The responsibility for the state of Chattisgarh lay on my shoulders. Calls, not only from Tiger Rana, but also from the National Sales Manager had become quite frequent. As I had been often reminded by Tiger Rana, I would have to either rise to the occasion or fall and bite the dust.

DKD was busy clearing some bills when I knocked on the door of his office.

'Sir namaskar,' he said, as he got up to open the door, 'why are you standing outside? Please, come in.'

He immediately ordered an assistant to scout for tea and *pakodi*s even as I walked in.

'How have you been, Dayal *saab*, and how is business?'

'As usual sir. Is anything ever hidden from you? You know what setbacks we faced in November, we are yet to recover from that. March is upon us, you know how high stakes are this time, do enlighten us how we can serve you.'

There was clearly a cold war raging between us which neither of us could afford to give fire to. We both needed each other. As long as I was in his territory no additional benefit could be passed on to him without my permission, even if Tiger Rana approved of it. He had seen it happen earlier. At the same time, as long as he was in my territory, there was no way I could have achieved my numbers without his cooperation. I had seen it earlier too. It was an unspoken truth. Even though it would exist stealthily beneath the surface, it would never come out into the open.

'Yes Dayal *saab*, stakes are higher this time,' I said, 'it's a tall peak we have to climb in March. Would you want to share any plans you might have?'

DKD gave me a broad smile. 'What can we dare to suggest when your good self is there to take care of us, sir?' he said, with a false smile on his face. 'But still sir, if you permit, I have made a plan. Please, excuse me for a minute, I will be right back.'

He went inside and fetched a pen drive to key into his computer. Even though the numbers racked up to Rs 1.5 crore for the entire state of Chattisgarh, for his territory of Raipur, Bhilai and Bilaspur they totaled a figure of Rs one crore. He had done the math; he knew how significant he was to us, particularly to me. To be honest, he had put in a good deal of hard work to devise the plan he was proposing. The whole area had been divided into zones and beats with revenue potential ascribed to each outlet, divided by stock keeping units. What could be pushed to whom, in what quantities and at what rates had been specified. The approach was logical and systematic. At the end of it all, he had put in a request for a bottom line figure of the estimated budget required for the complete plan and execution, a figure that glared unabashedly at me from the glittering computer screen – 14% of total sale value.

'This is insane Dayal *saab*,' I exclaimed. 'An estimate of 14%? Last year, we had achieved all our targets within 12%. I appreciate the effort you have put in to make this plan, but the figure you put up is preposterous. My estimate of the market is 10%. I don't think there is any need for unnecessary expenditure.'

'You are right sir, last year we had achieved our numbers within 12%. But last year our targets were 50 lakhs. Look at what you are expecting this year, one crore – that is 100% growth, double the business. It is not that children have started eating more candy and mint, is it? In fact they now run away from it. What damage it is causing to their teeth and health you know. Even I keep my son away from it as much as possible. I give him a beating if I find him sucking a mint behind my back. Where will we get this extra business from, then? From the competitors isn't it? We would have to loosen our pockets, I am telling you beforehand. Don't blame me later if we are unable to meet our numbers.'

I knew this was nothing but a trick to wheedle as much as he could from the company. I didn't want to create another Raju Seth situation by falling short on the numbers. That was a much bigger a risk to take than shelving a few extra bucks on DKD. Besides, Tiger Rana was anyway agreeable to the idea, I thought. It was grossly unfair but I had no choice. We negotiated and finally closed the discussion on 12%. He had a sly smile on his face; we both knew he was having the last laugh. I clenched my teeth in helplessness and gulped down my anger with the hot tea and *pakodi*s.

***

Three months had gone by, and Raju Seth was still sitting at dues of Rs 13 lakhs. IOC had started charging him interest on a daily basis. The dreaded knock of the insurers was lurking around the corner. More than that, head office had advised blocking all transactions beginning the following week. A blocked customer, fall in sales and the mound of debt to be buried under, the situation didn't augur well for a fruitful tomorrow.

A discussion with Ramteke revealed that he still had nearly ten lakhs worth of excess stock lying in his godown. With season sales round the corner, liquidation would have become easier. But in case the company decided to block his accounts before that, shipments to the market would be stopped, circulation of money would be seriously hampered. Once the rotation stopped I knew the market would hold back all its payments, the working capital flow would dry up and it would become even more difficult to clear the dues. I had to keep the clock ticking for at least two more weeks, till the peak season kicked in, and the only way out was to take back Ramteke's excess stocks, and reduce his debt. I put forth a request to Tiger Rana.

'What is this Sanjay?' he enquired, as he laid his eyes on my application, 'you propose to return the sold stocks from Jagdalpur?'

'He is sitting on an outstanding of Rs.13 lakhs sir, there is excess stock lying in his godown. The customer will get blocked if we don't take this step right now, and that will further worsen the situation.'

'We are almost in the midst of season, we have a high peak to conquer, and you are telling me instead of selling more I should take stock back? You must be the first sales manager who has had the wit and the audacity to make such a ridiculous suggestion, young man!'

I let the satire pass. 'Sir, this is the same stock we had billed him for in November end, when we were falling short of our numbers, remember? Even then I had said, the quantity is more than the potential of the town, but you asked me to go ahead.'

'Careful soldier, don't drag me down into your mess!' His voice rose several decibels. 'The customer is sitting on three months of debt and you come up with your brilliant idea today? If he was not going to be able to pay for what he was buying, he should have known. I can't force anyone, can I? I can't put a gun to anyone's head and ask him to concede a sale, can I? More so than him, your salesman should have known, you should have known. What amazes me is how you could even take such an irresponsible decision.'

'But sir', I countered, 'you had asked me to go ahead with it to rack up the 100%. I was against the idea from the very beginning.'

'Do you have that in writing?' he shot back.

'Not in writing sir but we had a discussion and...'

'This is your territory Sanjay, for better or worse,' he said, qualifying my protest, 'you call the shots here. You said you didn't wish to give DKD an extra 2%, I said fine, no issues. You said you wanted to splurge 1% on salesman incentives. I was against the idea from the very beginning. Yet, did I not give you the nod? I did. The only thing I told you was that I want the numbers on my desk, you decide the way you want to plan it, I won't object. If you give additional credit to a customer beyond his capacity, it's your decision, it's your market, you should know him better than anyone else, shouldn't you? And today when the cat is out of the bag, you come back and put this all on my head? I won't call it unprofessional, I'd say it is just plain dumb. I would even call it cowardly.'

I remained silent, stunned by his response, by his complete turnaround on his words. I still didn't know where I had gone wrong.

'I want this set straight by this week end,' he continued, firm and clear in his tone and words. 'This is a grave matter, Sanjay, very grave. A bad debt of thirteen lakhs is not a joke, and the axe will fall on you, no one else. Not on your salesman, he just executes the plans you make, not on me or NSM or anyone else, the territory lies in your jurisdiction. This is what you supposedly blue eyed boys are for, aren't you? To make decisions. To make correct, fruitful, insightful decisions that benefit the organization, not the ones that run money down the drain. Indiscreet decisions like these will not be taken lightly, is that understood?'

'I understand sir', I said dejectedly, as I got up to leave.

'What is the budget plan for DKD this season?' he enquired.

'12% sir,' I answered, 'we do hope to crack the numbers this time around.'

He smiled. 'Good, you do show rare glimpses of improvement. You can leave now.'

I walked out with my tail right between my legs.

***

That night I received a text message from Sagar Shah. 'Hi Sanjay, haven't heard from you, how is your script going?'

Sagar had expected me to pen down and send him the first draft by January, latest by February. This was March, and all I had till date were five pages, two scenes in total, plus a medley of random thoughts. The next twenty days or so were going to be extremely hectic owing to season sales and my performance graph was nowhere near touching the skies. I didn't know when I would be able to take time out to write.

After a moment's thought, I replied, 'In progress. Have been considerably busy past few days in office owing to financial year end. Should be ready with the first draft by April.'

I was buying two months more time from a director who would have scripts like mine from nobodys like me dumped into the trash can in a corner of his room. This is my dream being held to ransom, I said to myself, and for what, to work fourteen hours a day for a paycheck that feels good when it credits into my account every month but robs me of my sleep for each of those thirty days? To earn some cherry points from Tiger Rana? Or to help the great and gargantuan IOC mint a million more bucks by selling mint? *After some time, it really becomes all about the money. They forget what they had told me the other night. They forget they had come to the city to swim.* I feared I was fast turning into the men in Ramteke's story. I was on two boats, each going in opposite directions. Either you choose one and set sail with the wind behind you or you muddle along with your feet between the two and try not to drown in the waters below. I made a resolution again that night: I will get past the season sales with a respectable achievement, with no further hiccups, and post that, I will sit down and write the script.

***

Baap had left IOC. Raagini was right; he wasn't given an official farewell. People like me who had been trained or mentored by him decided to put together a small gathering for him on their own. Even though I should have been the host, I was in the invitees list. Invited by Karan and Raagini. Especially by Raagini, she insisted I should come, for Baap. I wanted to go but couldn't. Tiger Rana didn't warm to the idea of multiple leaves within a week. He didn't really care who Baap was, he didn't report to him.

She called me a few days later.

'Baap is gone Sanjay, he left. This plant will never be the same again,' she said, referring to the factory we both used to work in.

'And who is going to replace him?' I asked.

'Sendu, who else,' she answered, 'he was the happiest of them all today. He now gets the top job.'

'And how is Baap?' I didn't know why I was feeling sympathetic towards him today.

'He tried to show that he was doing great, but I don't think he was', she replied. 'It seemed as if there is a dark animosity prevailing between him and the Chairman. He even threw in a few derogatory remarks casually. We could feel the love lost between them.'

'For a man of that stature, to denigrate another celebrated, highly regarded colleague, that too in public? Isn't it strange?' I said.

'Everyone has a breaking point Sanjay,' she remarked, 'everyone.'

Prioritize, she had said. After a long and uncomfortable silence, she spoke again.

'I am thinking of leaving this place. It won't be the same from now on.'

'Leaving? Why? What about your job?' I asked, surprised.

'I might look for something in Delhi or Mumbai,' she replied. 'My parents want me to shift. They say Puneet will be working in either of these two cities.'

'Puneet?' The very mention of his name set my heart on fire. 'What about him?'

'Nothing about him. He is coming to Chennai in some days. He has some work and our parents want us to meet. I might run away, leave the city on some work trip myself.'

'I meant,' I reiterated, 'why should your moving from Chennai have anything to do with *him*? You said you don't like him, right?'

'I don't, and it is not related to him, it is just one of the things in their consideration set,' she stated. 'But then Sanjay, what other option do I have?'

My heart jostled with my mind to find an answer. Is this really what she wants to hear or is it just a figment of my imagination, reading between the lines? Is it too early to make a decision, too premature to ask for an answer? I don't yet know where I am going with my career, if I am going anywhere at all. What if I do happen to write the script, will I be able to continue with my job? What is the guarantee that my script will take me somewhere worthwhile? Where will the paycheck come from? Can I take up a responsibility? Or would it be unfair on my part to disrupt another world for my castle of cards? Is it not better to go with the flow, and let the tide of time find its own favour? What if we sleep over it and start all over? I let the question hang in the air, for another tomorrow.

CYA AND PTS

Cover your Ass and Pass the Shit

Time does not walk. It does not crawl, run, ride a bus, jeep or train. Time flies. The next twenty days flew in the blink of an eye. It was the 28th of March, three days before the annual closing, the deadline. Raju Seth had been blocked. His stock was stuck in his godowns, his money in the market. There had been no sale in Jagdalpur market for the whole month, leaving a shortfall of 15 lakhs of business staring me in the face. Tiger Rana was clear in his verdict. I can take fire from a cannon, soldier, but I won't accept a fall in numbers. To achieve One Crore, DKD had filed another request for extension of credit from two months to three, which had been sanctioned. He was now my only hope, my saving grace. I sat there in his office sipping tea and eating pakodis.

'We have achieved ninety lakhs Dayal *saab*,' I stated, 'ten more in the next three days, and…maybe if we could push it further?' I was almost pleading.

'As long as we have your blessings sir, we are your servants.' That smile was so insincere, it made me feel small.

'If I may ask sir,' he continued, 'what's been happening in Jagdalpur? I heard about the problems Raju Seth has been going through.'

'It's highly unfortunate Dayal *saab*. We gave him credit which he has not been able to pay back in time. About ten lakh worth of stock is lying idle. The market is not clearing the dues. You know the drill, you know what happens when a businessman goes out of business.'

'I know sir, this is highly unfortunate,' he said repeating my words. 'And something like this happening to a person like Raju Seth, it's tragic,' he stated shaking his head sympathetically. 'What are we doing now in his market? You must be facing a severe loss in sales, isn't it?'

'Yes, Dayal *saab*, you are absolutely right. Not a single unit has been shipped to Jagdalpur till now, no sale for the entire month. The market is clamoring for stocks but Raju Seth can no longer supply. His dues to the company have to be cleared first. It's a complete mess,' I said, throwing up my hands in exasperation.

'There could be a solution sir, if I may suggest,' he said a few minutes later.

'What Dayal *saab*? What possible solution could there be?' Is DKD going to be kind enough to offer monetary help to Raju Seth, I wondered, and wished he would.

'Do you want to meet your targets Sanjay sir?' The question was direct.

'Of course, Dayal *saab*, I definitely do, and I also wish Raju Seth comes out of this mess.'

'Forget Raju Seth for a moment,' he interjected, 'you have to meet your targets right? I have a way by which you can do that.'

'What is that?' I asked moving to the edge of my chair filled with curiosity. I would have grabbed any straw that was thrown to me at that moment.

'You say Raju Seth has ten lakhs worth of stocks lying idle in the godowns, right? He won't be able to sell it unless he is unblocked and provided further stock to restart the rotation. But for you to get your numbers, you don't need to necessarily sell it, just show it on paper.'

'Show it on paper? What do you mean?'

'Your data monitoring system is currently showing this stock as idle, unsold in the system. Just show the idle stock as sold, on paper, in the system, not in reality. No one will come to know unless someone does a physical check, which in this case, seems highly unlikely.'

'But that will be fraud, Dayal *saab*!' I couldn't believe what I was hearing.

'Yes it would be, but only if someone ever comes to know about it, isn't it? If Raju Seth remains blocked, this secret goes with him to his grave. Also, please allow me to supply stock from here to Jagdalpur. You know there is demand in the market. If you say yes, I will ship stocks worth fifteen lakhs tomorrow. I would request your good self to pay me an additional 2% on that. You will meet your targets. Both of us will celebrate a happy year ending!'

'Dayal *saab*, what are you saying? It will completely destroy the Jagdalpur market. If they get stock from you, no retailer will ever pay back Raju Seth. He will be ruined.'

'This is business sir. Please, we are all professionals, it's not about emotion. Raju Seth is my dear friend of course but business must not be mixed with emotions, isn't it? And you meet your targets, sir. That's what you want, right?'

'What if someone finds out Dayal *saab*?' I asked apprehensively.

'You think this is the first time I am suggesting such a thing Sanjay ji? You are new, you feel frightened. It happens all the time. Someone has to lose for someone to win. And then, why do you worry, you are going to get transferred from here next month, even if someone finds out, you will be gone by then! It won't be your headache any more. I have seen how these things function here sir, I am just offering you some fatherly advice.

You should remember it. It will come in handy throughout your life. You cover your ass and pass the shit.'

The offer was tempting. I was caught in a whirlpool and this seemed the only way to bail out. DKD is right, I will be transferred next month anyway. Then it will be the headache of the person who takes over. Why should I lose my sleep over it? I shall meet my numbers and also come out clean on the other side. Raju Seth is not a rookie. He has managed all his life, he will manage in the future too. I don't need to worry about the whole world while my own house is on fire.

'There is one more issue that would need to be resolved sir,' he said, breaking into my stream of happy thoughts, 'Ramteke. He would come to know. And he is the only one who would actually have to fudge the sales, because it is his territory, am I right?'

I nodded. I would have to ask Ramteke to do it.

'Has he done such a thing before?' I enquired.

'No sir, not Ramteke. Many others have. But everyone assumes he won't cooperate, so they won't approach him. But as both of us can see, what option do you have anyway?'

The next day I flew to Jagdalpur. Time was running out. Only two days left before D-day. My first objective was to meet Raju Seth. Persuade, plead, cajole, threaten, delude, deceive, use any trick in the book to make him remit his outstanding amounts. That would have served my purpose without having to resort to any underhand means.

I never wanted to act on DKD's suggestions, it was completely against my principles. Ramteke was on brink of a promotion. A loss in sales and a blocked customer would have created hindrances, but a fraud could have cost him his job. I knew it, Ramteke knew it, DKD knew it. Ramteke had a family to feed – his parents, wife, three children. Mahesh had only very recently started working and the remuneration was nothing to boast about. Moreover, Ramteke was not just my subordinate, he was a friend, the person who had mentored me during the early days, my philosopher, my guide.

I didn't want my actions to cause hardship to Raju Seth either, not that they hadn't already. The decision to ship him excess stocks was mine. Today, times were tough, but if only we could hang on, there could be hope for a better tomorrow. I didn't want to be the one to destroy his market and ruin his business. He was an honest man, a good man, unlike the manipulative diabolical DKD.

I didn't want to do any of these things, I honestly didn't, but Tiger Rana wanted the numbers at any cost. I had no choice, no choice at all. Only a few days ago I had made a resolution to myself, *I will get past the season sales with a respectable achievement and no further hiccups, and post that, I will get down to creating the script.* My calling card was beckoning me, all I needed to do was ensure that my safety net remained safe. After that I would commit myself to my script. Ah! how great a feeling that would be! I wanted no bouquets, no, not at all, I didn't want someone to come and congratulate me on my achievement or anything like that, but I didn't want any brickbats either. Honesty is a concept born more out of convenience and circumstance. Not speaking the truth is not lying, no one has to know. Step aside and let the storm pass. Just two more days, one quick decision and all this will be over.

'Sir, welcome back!' Ramteke's greeting was effusive as I stepped into Raju Seth's shop. 'We thought you might just leave the state without meeting us again. But you didn't. That's very good of you sir.'

Raju Seth gave me a warm smile and asked me to sit down. I wished to God he would not make it tougher than it already was.

It was peak business hours in the evening, but the shop was emptier than usual. There were no long queues of customers as there used to be. It was evident business was down.

'Sir,' began Raju Seth, 'before you say anything else, I have something to say.'

'What is it Raju Seth?' I asked apprehensively.

'I have some good news and some bad news. What would you want me to go with first?'

'First the bad news and then the good one,' I replied, hoping the bad news was not what I didn't want to hear.

'The bad news, sir, is that I am terribly sorry. I don't know how to say this to you, but I just won't be able to clear my dues this month. I have some limitations which I know are excuses and I can only curse myself for that. But I feel really ashamed that due to me you are facing such difficulties. I know I have not been able to give you any business this season, and what adverse impact that has had on you. When I see good, honest men like you who have a clean heart, it makes me feel good, it tells me not everything is lost in this world and there is still hope. But when such a person has to suffer because of me, it only makes me hang my head in shame. Please sir, I am making arrangements, next month for sure. I have some old property we are trying to sell. But this month, there is nothing I can do.'

After this long speech, all my plans of pleading, cajoling, threatening, deceiving…using any trick fell flat. I just didn't know how to do that anymore. The biggest problem was that he sounded genuine about what he said.

'What is the good news Raju Seth?' I asked.

He gave both Ramteke and me one of his heartiest smiles. 'Sanjay ji', he said, 'it seems there might just be a solution in sight in our battle. There is hope that the naxals might want to surrender.'

'Give up arms?' I asked surprised, 'What are you saying Raju Seth?'

'It seems likely, sir,' said Ramteke, 'Mahesh told me the other day. There have been talks going on between the CRPF and the naxal leaders for about a month now. It is not in the media yet, so nobody knows about it. The CRPF has kept the whole operation under wraps to prevent publicity, or any kind of hype. They can't risk a rumor spreading before something concrete actually happens. There could be a meeting soon, one last one, between the CRPF and the naxals, where the issue will be resolved and they will give up their arms. And sir,' he beamed proudly, 'Mahesh might also be a part of this operation.'

It was indeed some exceptional news. It was their dream, Mahesh's dream. Something they were living for, something that could actually happen soon. I congratulated them and wished for a peaceful, happier tomorrow.

After the pleasantries, I wanted to come down to business, the reason I had visited the town. Talking to Raju Seth did not appear to provide any solution, and my last resort to implement DKD's suggestion seemed inevitable. I looked for an opportunity to talk to Ramteke in private.

'There are only two days left Ramteke, is there nothing we can do?' I asked.

'There is a huge demand in the market, sir. I have been assuring them we shall supply soon,' he said. 'You know we have good relations with all the retailers. They want to buy from us, not touch the competition. But what can I do if we can't supply?'

'Raju Seth just told me his situation, Ramteke, tell me something I already don't know.' My voice had risen sharply. 'I know *he* can't supply. How much stock does he have in his godowns you told me?'

'Worth about ten lakhs sir,' he answered.

'Tell me Ramteke, meeting our numbers this month is crucial from me. Is there *anything* we can do?'

Ramteke looked directly into my eyes. He knew what I meant, what I intended to say but had not put in words. I don't know what thoughts were running through his mind as he stood there quietly for a minute and continued to stare at me. I felt as if his gaze had pierced right through me, my clothes, my skin and my chest as I stood naked in front of him, baring body and soul. I felt weak in my knees and wretched in my spirit.

'What exactly do you mean sir?' he said.

He wanted me to say it, put it in words. *A fraud could have cost him his job, I knew it, he knew it.* He was not afraid of that, both of us knew that as well. But there are some things some men just can't do. There is no reason to it, it's not about having principles that are sacrosanct, or about the false pride one boasts of to convey one's uprightness in social gatherings. It's not about whether the world mocks or appreciates, it's just that some things some men cannot do. It's the way they are made.

That day and that hour, Ramteke made me realize I was not one of those men. I might have wanted to delude myself and feel happy about it, but I was an opportunist hoot who squeals when his tail is caught in the woods. And that is why I would never be able to shed the fear of failure and have the courage to pursue my dreams. I would never be able to think beyond my safety net. I couldn't ask him to do what I had come for. I wished the peace operation good luck, bid good bye and left.

MAHESH SANGLI

Who my friend has won the race?

1 April 2010

April 1 is the most significant day in the life of any organization. It marks the end of the year gone by and heralds the onset of the coming one. It is on this day that the books are closed and balance sheets matched, when computers finally throw up the revenues and profits raked in by the organization in the course of the year. Maybe that is why it is called the April Fools' Day.

I walked into office that day with my head hanging and my feet faltering, fearing severe ridicule and castigation from Tiger Rana. The sales figures would get keyed in by noon and they would bring my ineptness out in the open, making me the one who would go going down in the history of IOC Foods as having delivered the worst performance in Chattisgarh. Fifteen lakhs short of 1.5 crore would mean only a 90% achievement. All the others were sure to fly way above me. Why did I not think of giving DKD his 2% in the very beginning, in the month of November? We would have met our targets, Tiger Rana would have been happy, there would have been no need to ship excess stocks on credit to Raju Seth, he would have never got blocked, and I would have been sitting pretty today on healthy figures. And what did I gain out of that act of indiscreet bravado? DKD anyway got the lion's share in March whereas I ended up in a complete mess.

Tiger Rana was a busy man that day. He was discussing with Regional Sales Managers from all over the country to see who had reached where. The top achiever all India got a generous salary hike plus a foreign tour and national acclaim at the annual conference five days later. After finishing with con-calls and video conferences, he got down to meeting his team, calling each of them into his cabin one by one. I was reserved for the last, for special treatment.

'Young man, he said, 'I have been dying to see you, where have you been? Come in.'

'I...I was here only sir, sitting in my cabin,' I stammered.

'Silent killer young man, the latent hero, what a miracle you have pulled off!' he said, beaming with joy.

'Er, umm, I don't understand sir,' I said, confused by his greeting. I wondered if the shock of my dismal performance was so great that it had unbalanced him.

'Have you not seen the final numbers?'

I had not, out of sheer trepidation. 'Sir, I...I just did and I am sorry but...' I was trying to construct a defence.

'Exemplary,' he interjected, 'scaling the peak like a true warrior should, 97% achievement, 145 lakhs! Superb show, you have made us all proud, Sanjay. We stand highest all India, and you, you have delivered the best results of all. It was very very close I must tell you, nearly everyone has gone past 90%. But then, only real heroes have it in them to climb the last few steps, don't they?'

I was astonished by his words, and perplexed by his statements. How could that have happened? 145 lakhs? I was pretty certain I was going to close at 135!

'The annual business conference is on 6th April. I am going to bring you on stage. You will receive the Best Employee of the Year award. You have done it my boy, you have done it! Congratulations!'

I was ecstatic to hear what Tiger Rana was saying, Best employee of the year award! And then I was going to get transferred, Utopia… However, slowly the thought began to rise from the depths of my conscience. Ramteke had keyed in the fraud sale! What would happen to him and Raju Seth once I was gone? And the money that lay in debt?

'Thank you very much sir,' I replied, swallowing hard. 'It has all been thanks to your guidance sir,' I lied. 'But I have one offhand question sir, if I may please.'

'What Sanjay? Ask me anything.'

'There are some outstandings in Jagdalpur you know, what do we do about that?'

'Petty issues, Sanjay, don't worry about it. We might reconcile the stock, do a physical check once and take it back, the insurers will recover the remaining debt. You don't worry, you only think about the 6th of April now, and your next posting!'

***

6 April 2010

It was my 24th birthday. The grand auditorium was filled with more than a thousand people that day. The CEO, the Senior Vice Presidents, the Presidents, heads of business groups, senior level managers, high profile leaders, middle level managers, new joinees, representatives from departments of research, human resource, operations, you name it, everyone was there in the hall. The atmosphere was electric, they were all elated by the exceptional results declared by IOC for the last financial year. Shareholder dividends had been announced to the tune of 20%. Employee salary increments by 25 % had been declared. People planned their vacations, the new vehicle they were soon going to buy or the home theatre that would adorn their living rooms.

'For exemplary display of leadership and managerial acumen, skill and ability,' said the compere as his voice echoed from all corners of the auditorium 'for best performance in the year 2009–10 and the future torchbearer of the glory of IOC, I wish to call upon stage, recipient of Best Employee of the Year Award 2009–10, Mr. Sanjay Saklani.'

I walked up to the stage amidst a thunderous applause. A thousand hands clapping in unison!

Congratulations, young man!

What is the secret of your success, mate?

Keep it up , you will make it big!

We need people like you, you are now an inspiration, a role model!

Enjoy the night, but don't rest on your laurels, from tomorrow, we want more!!

Karan, too, was there and came up to congratulate me. 'Proud of you man. The way you started, I didn't expect you would make it.'

'Well, didn't you say once' I replied with a big beaming smile on my face, 'the big O that's called Outstanding? Promotion in three years, salary doubles in five. Every goddamn HR in the country would want to snap me up.'

> Who is the one that beats all odds? Sanjay, Sanjay…clap, clap, clap
> Who is the one that calls the shots? Sanjay, Sanjay…clap, clap, clap
> Who is the one that leads the chase? Sanjay, Sanjay…clap, clap, clap
> Who my friend has won the race? Sanjay, Sanjay…clap, clap, clap
> Who my friend has won the race? Sanjay, Sanjay…clap, clap, clap
> Who my friend has won the race? Sanjay, Sanjay…clap, clap, clap

CHORUS. BLACK OUT.

***

It was Amavasya, the night of the new moon. They said they had never seen a night as dark as this. The stars which should have been shining brightly had hidden behind clouds. Lights were beginning to fade in the village of Geedum. Night camp had been set up. One hundred and twenty CRPF men sleeping under the sky, waited for tomorrow. Tomorrow, a Special Task Force meeting with top Naxal leaders was scheduled in Dantewada. A team of twenty men had been specifically assigned the task. Negotiate, talk, discuss, argue, come out with a resolution – No Arms. The remaining hundred were to hold anchor in Geedum, await their unit's victorious return or if things got ugly, march.

Ramteke lay on his bed waiting for sleep. The limbs were tired, the mind was restless, the eyes wide open. Why wouldn't the God of sleep sneak into his room and rob him off his senses? The night must tick away the hours. He kept staring at the clock by his bedside: 11.00 pm, six more hours to dawn. A few minutes later, he got out of bed and began to pace up and down the room, rubbing his hands together. He didn't know why he was feeling so anxious. Tomorrow was the day of truth, the day of reckoning and change, the harbinger of a new dawn, a better dawn for everyone. They stood on the cusp of history. Six more hours before dawn, the night must pass.

The silence of the night was disturbed by the rustling of leaves. The steps were small, but great in number. Their faces were masked by paint and the hands were armed with spears and bows. The rustling entourage broke the hush as the painted faces encircled the camp, their wide eyes scanning the lamps on the tents and the cats on the prowl for any kind of movement. There was none.

Their platoon leader took a pair of binoculars to survey the posts in the distance, and for hidden barricades, snipers at a height, dogs on the leash. Four check posts were identified, one in each direction that secured the area. He signaled with his hands and eyes, ordering the men to form four small teams of four men each. These teams were ordered to advance to the check posts while the rest of the platoon waited behind the bushes. One, two, three, four...throats were slit without a squeak as the men lay amidst pools of blood, on the ground. The signal was given, all posts cleared, time to march. The platoon leader ordered his men in, all forces together, from all directions, the attack must be sudden and lethal.

'It's an ambush', they shrieked, as the pall of death descended over the sleeping CRPF men. 'SECURE, FIGHT, RUN, It's an ambush' they screamed.

There was no time to do either. Their arms were chopped off before they could reach for their weapons. Their eyes were gouged out before they could take aim. Some fought valiantly in vain, some succumbed abjectly without a fight, some fled into obscurity. Mahesh raced to the eastern check post to grab his rifle and the knife. It was their weakest link, he figured. He hid behind the sand bars taking aim. Shot, one down, and then another. The fingers pressed the trigger as the eyes followed the targets. They were too many of them, hundreds, maybe even a thousand. The last twenty minutes of his life, that's what he had lived for since the last twenty years of his life. He fought gallantly under the skies, a battle of blood to bring peace. Don't run, fellow men, the weak shall plunder you with their weapons, but the strong shall counter with their will. Keep faith fellow men, don't run. He died a valiant death.

Seventy six CRPF men were killed that night, in one of the most gruesome guerilla attacks by the naxals. Seventy six men striving for peace butchered in their sleep, punished for an offence they had not committed. Seventy six men who went to bed just like the million others that night, but would never wake up to witness another dawn. The end of their dreams, their desires, their safety nets and their calling cards. No second chance, no time to make amends, no allowance to live another day to wipe off any regrets or fulfill any wishes that might have been left in their hearts. Seventy six men who lived for their purpose, and died for the same.

***

The next morning I woke up with a bad hangover. The booze, the fame and the accolades were still ringing in my head. Twenty three days were left to the end of April, and I still hadn't written a word more. I no longer had the inclination. It seemed too laborious to toil that hard. I picked up the newspaper and lumbered along to the pot. The headline was gory and so were the pictures. Was it still the hangover or was it for real? I flipped hastily to the fourth page for detailed information. It carried the names of the dead, no. 47, Mahesh Sangli, Village Geedum, Dantewada.

I thought I would throw up. *I want to bring peace Sanjay ji, in our homes, in our village, in our lives.* I wanted to call Ramteke. What would I say to him? He had lost his son, the future of his khandan, the bread-earner in his family. I had put Ramteke's job in jeopardy. He went ahead with it even though he knew the consequences. I had been selfish asking him to do it, to remain protected in my safety net, procrastinating my dreams, forfeiting my conscience.

I was not the one who had killed Mahesh that night, but I don't know why somewhere I felt responsible, somewhere I felt mocked by his purpose and his conviction. Here was a man who had given up his life for his dream and I was the one still thinking about it, finding excuses for not pursuing it, clinging to my safety net... *One man with courage is an army, isn't it?* I felt guilty celebrating the success I didn't deserve. I felt guilty for calling myself a friend of someone who I was willing to let suffer for my own weaknesses. He hadn't thought twice before sacrificing himself for me. I felt guilty for reveling in the fame and applause that I had sold myself for. I was the man of the moment in IOC, yet I don't know why, I felt shallow, I felt helpless. I felt I was a coward. I looked in the mirror and hated myself.

Fifteen months after that day I had done the unthinkable.

PART III

THE CALLING CARD

"There are some people who live in a dream world, some who face reality, and then there are those who convert one into the other"

FIFTEEN MONTHS LATER

Tough week this, man, rent bhi dena hai

It was around 6 pm. I was sitting on the railing of the balcony of Vinay's fourth floor apartment near Vile Parle station, dangling my faded Levis-clad legs over the railing. The evening sky was a palette of colours – pink, gold, purple. The sun wearing his dusky orange hat was bidding goodbye to another day. He had done his job well. The spring was marching by ushering in the summers of Mumbai.

A few blocks away, some kids were playing on the street, an old game I remembered from childhood – Kho Kho. Members of one team sat on their haunches, while one of them chased the member of the other team. Every time the 'den' patted a team mate's back and said 'kho' everyone would scream hysterically. But the one being chased was no easy catch. He had deceptively sharp moves and ran faster than the others. The team kept pegging each other, kho-kho-kho kho-kho. A sharp pass was all that was needed, the right timing. I realized I was leaning forward, and shouting along with them, Come on, Kho..NOW! Just then, I heard the door open behind me. Vinay had come in. It was good to see him after so long.

'*Pair latka ke baitha hai, gir jaega.*' (you are leaning so precariously, you can fall over)

'*Gir bhi jaunga to kya ho jaega yaar, abhi kaunsa thik se khada hun.*' I said. (What difference will it make even if I fall, yaar… I am not standing firmly as it is)

He laughed, looking straight at me as we embraced. 'Get ready, put on a shirt, we are going to Prithvi.'

'Vinay,' I replied, 'I don't know what I am doing, man. I really don't. I fear I might have made the biggest mistake of my life.'

There was a huge roar behind us. My attention got diverted from Vinay briefly. The children were yelling in wild jubilation. Apparently, they had caught the runner. He had made a mistake, taken a wrong turn, and bang, got caught. The game was over. Soon, they rearranged themselves and had a new den. Once again they were on their haunches, ready to set off the moment they felt the thump on their backs accompanied by a loud, 'Kho!' It was a new chase, a new game.

Vinay was a batch-mate from my MBA college. He was not just a batch-mate, he was a friend, a good friend. In fact we were even flat-mates two years ago. We shared similar interests, and had been on the stage a few times. He was a brilliant writer, not was, still is, only, I wouldn't know. I had not seen him for quite a while. Both of us had started off together with a burning desire to do theatre in the first year. He would write the scripts, I would lead the team and we would do the direction. As time went by, I dived deeper into my marketing projects, he immersed in his writing. I too wanted to, but it required a lot of patience and I wasn't sure it would earn me a living, so why the pain, I told myself. By the time we passed out from college, I had great projects, a great internship opportunity, great achievements and a great IOC offer under my belt. He had few random pieces of musings and a silly Day 3 startup just enough to pay his bills.

'*Two cutting chai,*' he said, gesturing to the waiter. We were sitting in Prithvi Café in the premises of the hallowed Prithvi Theatre, Juhu. Opposite the entrance yet not too far inside, the seats we chose gave us a panoramic view of the whole arena.

Chattering groups of friends, couples romancing over a cup of tea, theatre personalities and cine stars lounging around, enthusiasts queuing up for the next show, patrons browsing in the quaint little book store, a struggling artist hoping to get an opportunity or a carefree musician playing a melody on his flute, everything felt just the same as I had left it. There was a cacophony of sounds and a commotion of thoughts, yet a silence I had missed for long. I felt as if I was home again.

'Thanks Vinay,' I said, raising my cup in acknowledgement.

'Don't mention it,' he smiled, like old times. It seemed like it was only yesterday that we were coming back from a late night rehearsal, and had stopped to have a sip before heading back home.

'It seems the addiction hasn't left you yet,' I said, trying to make conversation, 'you still in love with Prithvi?'

'I think Prithvi is in love with me Sanjay. No matter how much I try, it just doesn't leave me.'

'We were all very impressed with you,' I said, 'when you preferred to take up a relatively lower CTC offer to remain in Mumbai and continue to serve your passion. It was inspiring.'

That was nothing but a white lie. At least until today, none of us were ever inspired by Vinay and whatever he had done with his life till now. Two years ago when we left college, he had one of the lowest offers during campus recruitment. And with time, it had only gone from bad to worse. I had heard that he had switched three jobs since then, none of them offering anything better. His job today too was not very impressive, not suited to his caliber, the institutes he had been educated in or the months of experience he had under his belt. His writing too wasn't going anywhere I was told. There were rumors that he was selling his poetry to whichever small publishers was willing to buy it, just to sustain himself.

'Hah,' he laughed, 'that's too generous of you. I would consider myself lucky if I was able to inspire even myself, let alone others! You were the big shot of campus, man', he said, shifting the focus of conversation towards me, 'Mr. Numero Uno, PPO from IOC, seven figure package, I heard you even got some sort of award within a year. Great going I must say. What happened then? Why suddenly this change? Are you jealous of your own self that you can't let him live in peace?'

'I don't know,' I said, anxious and unsure of myself, 'the money was good, the perks were amazing, the future looked bright, no doubt. But there was something missing. Somehow, I didn't love what I was doing, or you can say, I had never dreamt of doing that while I was a child. I had different ambitions Vinay, and I just didn't see myself fulfilling them if I continued doing what I was doing. Something had to change.'

Something had to change. Seven days ago, I was earning ninety thousand per month, stayed in five star hotels and travelling business class. I had spent two years working in FMCG sales, and was doing really well. An outstanding appraisal, employee of the year award, a star performer accreditation. Climbing my way swiftly up the ladder, I was living the corporate dream. Yet today I was unemployed.

'It was the money I think. I couldn't resist the temptation at that time,' I continued, 'I don't know how it happened. It was all good in the beginning. New and exciting, lot of status and all the luxury. But as months passed I felt as if I had begun to lead a life where I came back home every night wondering what it would be like if I didn't have to go back to work the next morning. I had begun to dread Mondays. Work became a burden, a routine, a day full of mundane activity with nowhere to go, nothing that would inspire. I was due for a promotion in a few months, Head of Zonal sales, a double raise, and an opportunity to work with the best in the industry. Yet, it did not excite me, the black hole within kept getting darker and deeper with each passing day. No real ambition, just a part on a conveyor belt, a cog in the wheel, a robot who has been programmed to do a certain set of actions that it keeps doing day after day after day…'

'I have had enough,' I said to Vinay, staring at the cup of tea lying on the table, 'I no longer want to compromise. I know I am afraid, but I know I am doing something I should have done a long time ago. For months I kept thinking, one day I will leave this place, go where I actually belong and live my dream, but I couldn't do it. Today, I am finally here, but my feet don't stand firm on the ground, my hands don't stay still. I don't know from where my next paycheck is going to come. All I know is that I want to get back to theatre, start a group, stage a production, do something meaningful, something that inspires me. I am ready to live on a pittance, but I want my life back. Don't get me wrong Vinay, please don't. But, but tell me, how do you do it?'

I thought he would take umbrage at the direct question. He just looked at me with a strange expression on his face. He waved to a person standing few feet away, apparently waiting for someone. The person waved back.

'How is it going?' Vinay called out to him.

'Bas yar, chal raha hai,' the person replied.

'Any luck yet?'

'*Nahin*, same old story. Let us see,' he said, bending his left knee to rest his back against the wall. 'Will be coming again on Monday I guess. Tough week this man, *rent bhi dena hai*.'

Someone who he was apparently waiting for appeared just then, so with a quick good bye he left. Vinay turned to me.

'You see that guy? He is a designer, wants to do costumes for the next Makarand Deshpande production. You will find him here nearly every second day. Have you ever worried about paying your rent Sanjay?' he asked.

'Not until now,' I replied.

'He has to, and I have to,' he said, 'it sounds great Sanjay, pursuing your passion, living the dream etc…etc, but you do a job to pay rent. I see you, and I think of myself two years ago. Even I was afraid. I took the road less travelled. Look at me today, I have no idea where I have reached. I still write, some scripts, few short stories here and there, it sounds very good to be creative and passionate and everything, but it takes a job to pay rent. That's what I have learnt.'

That indeed, was the cruel truth. No matter how much we watch fairytale movies about the hero pursuing his heart and living happily ever after, no matter how much we blame society or our education system for stifling our dreams and ruining our free spirit, the rules of the world remain the same for everyone. We can either accept them and find a way out to follow our heart or simply make excuses and find a shoulder to cry on. I knew it, Vinay knew it. His words were coming out of reality and experience, not frustration.

'You told your parents about your decision?' he asked, breaking the silence.

'Of course I did,' I replied. 'Our parents always support us in our dreams I realized. They love us, they don't have a choice. It is we who are weak inside, and we defend ourselves by shifting the blame of our cowardice on our parents. I will struggle with you. And I will find some job as well, here, in Mumbai. You know your love for theatre is still alive, isn't it? We will work it out together.'

'Like me, like that guy you just saw, every second person you will see here is a struggler,' he said. 'All of them are exceptionally talented. There are so many theatre groups out there, all vying for attention in the rapidly shrinking space. You find some energy in Prithvi or some fervor in NCPA but other than that? Theatre is gasping for breath and you want to jump in?'

'All through the last two years I have done the same thing,' I said, exasperated. 'Look at the market size, see how lucrative it is, how strong the competitors are, do a SWOT, what is the cost benefit ratio, what is the break-even, will the market respond, how to design my offering to suit the market, and everything else that told me to take action only where it promised profits, please the world around me. We are drawn to existing competitions like moths to a flame. Should we do something just because it is the popular thing to do or because we actually want to do it?'

I lowered my voice and tried to speak calmly. 'I am done toeing the line Vinay, I am done with that. If that's what I wanted, I could have happily continued in that fancy job doing what I was doing. I don't care where theatre is going man, I only know I want to be a part of it.'

'It will help you pay your bills Sanjay, that's all I am saying,' he said, patting me gently. 'I don't want you to repeat the mistakes I have committed.'

'How much will this Creator Labs job pay?' I asked, holding the letter in my hands.

'Junior Copywriter? Industry standards would be around 20–25 thousand per month I think. But this is not a very large organization it seems, and you have zero experience, so expect something in the range of 15–20 thousand. And trust me,' he broke this down for me as bluntly as he could, 'keeping aside your savings, you will not be able to survive in Mumbai on that salary.'

Survival of the fittest, wrote Charles Darwin. The lion with the loudest roar, the peacock with the prettiest feathers, the giraffe with the longest neck – Every species has its ways of survival and extinction. Those who can't cope with the tides of time, perish, be it the mighty dinosaurs or the giant mammoths. In the land of men, it was the man with the fattest wallet that was deemed the fittest, and survived.

I didn't tell Vinay, but over the past 15 months my savings had considerably dwindled. After insurers knocked down Raju Seth's shop and Ramteke lost his job, I used part of the money to help Raju Seth revive his business and part to help Ramteke get back on his feet. Today, I needed the money. I should probably take what Vinay was suggesting as a day job, a 9 to 5 kind of thing like Sagar Shah during the early days, I said to myself. It would help me stay afloat and I could use the remaining hours in more meaningful tasks, just like he did.

***

You were with IOC earlier Sanjay? The interviewer behind the table had raised the question. I replied in the affirmative. Why did you decide to quit? he asked. I couldn't tell him the truth. Why would he bother to hire me for if he came to know I had actually relocated to Mumbai to chase a wild and distant dream and was considering this job only as a paycheck, I thought. I stated personal reasons.

Why are you considering *this* job? He raised an eyebrow. He said I had better education, better experience and better credentials than required for the assignment he had to offer. He said I should look for better opportunities in bigger organizations with broader work profiles. He said I didn't belong there, that I wouldn't be satisfied with my role in his company and would soon quit out of frustration. He also said I wouldn't face much difficulty getting a better job, he was confident about it. Truth was I didn't want a better job; it would entail more responsibility and consume more time. And time was of the essence. I knew I had to lie again. What kind of excuse could I give to him if not to tell the truth?

An interview teaches us to lie. Lie well, as if you mean each and every word of it. The wise men sitting on other side of the table wish to hire men with ethics. You have to lie smart to show them you have ethics, and they will hire you. Like the devil, the key to a good lie is in the details, like dates or places. As an employee, lying is a core trait. Lying is indispensable. To boss, to subordinates, to peers, to vendors, to dealers, to everybody, to yourself. Day in and day out. A good liar makes a good employee, a good professional. People respect him, he brings accolades to the company. He goes on to rise up the ladder and one day hires new employees. They must have ethics, he insists.

I couldn't convince them with my lies. I must have committed forgery in my last organization and was forced to resign, they conjectured, else no sane person would make such a move. I respect their hypothesis, it's a valid hypothesis. I also couldn't tell them where I saw myself five years down the line. In a utopian world I would have wished to see myself staging my productions. I wouldn't know. As of now, I was jobless since two months, I didn't know where I saw myself five days later. I couldn't tell them that. Nor could I tell them what my passions and interests were. That's not what they wanted to listen to. They asked me to cite an example where I had gone out of my way to stick to an honest path in the midst of a tough situation. I had a bunch of examples where I had done the opposite. I wanted to tell them all those decisions led to good business growth, they said this was a question on honest paths and I must stick to it. Questions on business growth are separate and I need to give separate examples for that. He does not have goals, they said, and he does not possess ethics, they concluded.

It's as difficult to come down the job ladder as it is to climb up, I discovered that day. No one wants you anywhere except where you fit. I walked out of their Peninsula Towers office in Lower Parel. It was a hot summer afternoon and the sun was beating down hard on the streets. I wanted to get to the local railway station, little less than a kilometre away.

I stood at the traffic signal waving my hands to flag down a taxi. No one would stop, even those which weren't occupied. The route to the station from this area was usually congested, traffic moving at an excruciatingly slow speed. I finally gave up and began to walk.

My clothes were drenched with sweat. I couldn't wear the same shirt again without washing it. While in IOC I had never needed to walk in the sun, an air conditioned cab was always on standby. I reached the station only to be greeted by a long queue. I stood at the back. I had not had lunch. I couldn't stay with Vinay for too long. He was going to get married the following month, so I would need a place of my own. The queue was moving along at a snail's pace, people getting tickets to their destinations one by one. What was my destination?

The platforms were congested with people clamoring for one square foot of space to stand on. Had I jumped the gun by quitting IOC? I wondered. Would it have been possible to work out a solution while still being there? I missed the comforts and the security. I didn't want to travel in the train, it was hot and crowded. I wanted to go back to my air-conditioned, chauffeur-driven car. But it was too late now. I was not even welcome in IOC's smaller clones, I was over qualified and directionless, as I had just been told, looked at with skepticism. Where was I headed? I had reached the counter, the ticket-man asked, Where to? Goregaon return, single, I replied.

***

I didn't think much of Suchitra Dhani when I first laid eyes on her. She was sitting in a small cabin inside a smaller office compound I had walked into. A young looking girl with a girl-next-door appearance, must be one of the employees, I had thought. The room must have been about eight feet by ten feet, with six more people seated in smaller cabins or cubicles. There was a diminutive staircase at one end of the premises. The twelve feet high roof had been used to create another floor, about eight feet above, literally an attempt to create space out of air. The first floor of the office, as it was, had four more people seated there working on their computers. If ever they wished to walk down, they had to crouch and crawl towards the staircase, there wasn't enough room to stand up.

The interior of the office was aesthetically decorated, even though the space was limited. There were posters on every wall, propounding ideas on creativity, innovation and free spirit, several of them hand made. I looked around to see if someone could guide me to the CEO, I had her letter in my hands. There was a peon standing beside the gate, he came up to me with a glass of water. I showed him the letter and was asked to wait. About fifteen minutes later, I was called into her cabin.

'Mr. Sanjay Saklani?' she asked, with a warm smile, 'please, have a seat.'

I sat down and passed her my resume and the response letter from Creator Labs.

'Good afternoon ma'am,' I said. 'You might remember I had sent an application for the post of creative head with Creator Labs about one month ago. Here is your letter in response.'

'You can call me Suchitra,' she replied, taking the letter from me. 'I remember it because of your profile. We find people like you with your kind of qualifications and experience generally on the client's side giving us orders, not so much with a job application!' she chuckled. 'What brings you here?'

'You'd mentioned in your letter that you were not looking for a Creative head in your organization right now. Would there be any change in status? I assure you I would be good for the task.'

'No offence Sanjay, but regardless of your resume, I would have to gauge for myself if you were good for the task or not,' she stated. 'Regarding the profile you ask for, we are still not open. It's a small agency right now. I myself act as the creative head.'

'Ok,' I replied briefly, and went quiet. I didn't know whether I should ask her for the junior copywriter's position she had mentioned in her letter. 'Do you have any previous experience in advertising?' she asked.

'No, no professional experience as such. Didn't get an opportunity ever. There is some writing experience from college you can say, but that's it.'

'I mentioned in my letter that I am looking for a Junior Copywriter. Do you want to consider that position?'

What was the harm in giving it a shot? I said to myself, I had come all the way anyway. Come to think of it, I might keep it as some part time thing to earn a few bucks, I thought. I replied with a tentative nod.

'Ok, good,' she replied. 'Look Sanjay, I don't really care what all you have in your resume. For you to be up to this task, you need to have a certain way of thinking. A copywriter's way of thinking. It should have imagination yet it should have an objective. I am going to give you a test, a copy test, if you really are serious about taking up this kind of a job. Only after I see what you come up with I will decide. Now, tell me, do you really want to consider this and take the test?'

A test? I had not given a test in ages. Especially not this kind, maybe since those extracurricular activities back in college. Would be fun, I thought. Bring it on.

'Yes, sure,' I replied. 'What is the test?'

'Do you smoke?' she asked.

I was a little taken aback by the question. What did my smoking/non-smoking habits have to do with the test? Or was she inviting me for a smoking-break to discuss this? It was one of the quickest ways to bond with the boss and peers back in IOC! You can't say anything about these professional, successful girls these days, I said to myself.

'I am a casual smoker,' I replied. I didn't really smoke too often but I was curious to see where she would go with this.

'Then that is even better,' she smiled. 'We have a pharmaceutical client. They have started a new initiative on anti-smoking. And we are developing a website for them, especially for this campaign. We also have to include a banner advertisement on anti-smoking on the site. Do you know what a banner advertisement is?'

'I have an idea,' I replied, 'an ad that runs on a website with multiple frames and in a loop, right?'

'Yes that is correct. The ad shouldn't be more than five to six frames long. Now for your test today what I want you to think about and come up with, is a punch line for this ad. An anti-smoking ad punch line. Something which hits the smoker right on his face. So you have to get into the shoes of an anti-smoker and devise a punch line with his conviction. Then come back to the smoker to see whether his conviction relates and connects with the ad you have made to be able to make a life changing decision. Do you understand me? You can take as much time as you like, the earlier the better. Have some water, use the loo, go for a walk, do whatever you want. I look forward to seeing what you come up with.'

Suchitra Dhani was born in a middle class family in the suburban town of Rajkot, located in south-west Gujarat. Like many others in the city, her father was a garments trader with a thriving business. When his daughters passed out of high school, he felt the bustling town of traders, no matter how kind and favourable it had been to him and his family, would not offer enough avenues to his girls for a quality education and exposure. The kind he would have liked. Therefore, one fine day he decided to shut shop in Rajkot and move to Mumbai with his family of four.

He set up his business from scratch in the new city, put his daughters into courses and institutes they wanted to attend. Suchitra, the younger of the two sisters went to the JJ School of Art in south Mumbai to pursue graphic design.

After her graduation, she joined a renowned advertising agency as junior visualizer and worked in the industry for four years. Like it is with success and people, good work begets good work. Suchitra knew her work well, knew people in the industry who knew her work well and had inherited her hard-working genes from her father.

She had first begun to freelance, engaging clients with quality in her work and delivering on timelines. Soon she took a loan and set up her own agency. Creator Labs was now a two year old company with a small yet dedicated team, boasting of some well known clients under its belt. And Suchitra Dhani, nearly the same age as me, was the Chief Executive Officer of Creator Labs, where I had now appeared for a job interview.

I learnt all this in course of time, and then I figured that that was the difference between her and me. When I first met her, she was a complete contrast to what I was at that time – confused, unsure and afraid.

'Suchitra, can I come in?' I was standing outside her cabin, about an hour later.

'Come in Sanjay,' she said. 'Have you done what I had asked you to do?'

'Yes, I hope so,' I replied. One was usually required to come up with at least three or four ideas to present to the superior or the client who would then choose what they liked the most. I had learnt that in IOC. Today, I had only come up with one.

'I have conceptualized one idea,' I said, 'which I believe strikes the chord and achieves our objective. But it's not just a punch line, I want to take you through with the whole concept and script of this advert.' I had given deep thought to the exercise and wanted to present the most effective idea rather than harp on few mediocre ones.

'Fair enough. So what have you thought?'

'It's a four frame banner,' I stated, using my hands to amplify the narration, 'in the first frame, there is a still of a fist fight between two hands. One of these hands is a strong, muscular human hand and the other one is a cigarette portrayed as a human hand. The copy reads – Some who seem strong. The second frame is in animated motion, where the cigarette fist is shown beating the human fist in the contest. Here the copy reads – Aren't strong enough. Third frame has the end visual of second frame in still, i.e. the human hand prostrate on the floor beaten by the cigarette hand, and the copy reads – Not a weak man's game. So in sequence, the three frames read – *Some who seem strong aren't strong enough. Not a weak man's game.* Now the final frame which reads the punch line – *Losers fume, winners quit.'*

I did a signoff as if I had just given the president's speech to a full house. The more I had thought about it, the more I loved my idea. I was pumped up. There was a childlike excitement in my speech and a sparkle in my eye. I had felt this way after a long, long time.

She sat there quietly for a few minutes. I was looking at her anxiously.

'I like it,' she said, finally breaking the silence.

I was ecstatic. I was happier than the day I had won the best employee award in IOC, or when I had crossed the revered one crore mark in sales for my territory, or when I was awarded with a promotion. I was happy just the way I was when Sagar Shah had once called for me and for the same simple reason – I had been given an opportunity and was being appreciated for something I was passionate about. Like the fulfillment a computer scientist gets after designing a code, an athlete after winning a race or a doctor after saving a life.

'I'd like to work here,' I blurted out, a broad smile on my face.

'I will also be glad to have you on board Sanjay,' she smiled back. 'How much were you expecting by way of remuneration?'

This was the tricky part. I couldn't tell her I was earning ninety thousand per month in my last job. She would administer a polite no and bid me good bye. I was new to this industry, I didn't really know the salary structures either. Only the vague figures Vinay had thrown at me. I thought it would be best to let her state a figure.

'How much would you be willing to offer, Suchitra?' I asked, throwing the ball in her court.

'Sanjay, I have seen your profile, and I know where you are coming from. That is why I wanted you to be sure of yourself, whether you really wished to give this a shot or not. I shall be honest with you. This is a different industry with different dynamics. And you don't have relevant qualifications or relevant experience. As per industry standards, the best I can offer you right now is Rs 20,000 per month fixed plus 25% in variable. Tell me, why do you want to join Creator Labs after leaving your previous plush job?'

Any other day, this would have been a typical interview question checking the interest level of an applicant towards a college, course or job. All through my life I had lied to this question. I had lied when I was asked why engineering, I had lied when I was interviewed for my first job in a software firm, I had lied when I was asked why MBA by the admission panel, I had lied when I was asked why IOC when I passed out. I had lied to the interviewers. I had lied to the world. I had lied to myself. Today, I didn't feel the need to lie.

'I love this work,' I replied, still beaming. "This is where my heart lies, this is what keeps me going. I know I had a plush job which I left and am still too scared of what I am going to do with my life now, but at this moment, today, I feel no regrets. I will take it.'

'Great, then, Sanjay, welcome to Creator Labs. I look forward to working with you,' she said. Then added, 'I like you. You are true to yourself.'

FAITH AND HOPE

Yahan koi saga nahin hai

'MHADA Signal, Andheri West,' I said, getting into the auto rickshaw.

'Are you sure you want to do this?' asked Vinay, getting in after me.

'Sure of what, Vinay? It's already a year late. If anything, I should have done this a long time ago. Now when I have finally been able to complete *Nametag*, you are asking me to reconsider? Why?'

'Because what you are doing today, I have been doing for the past two years. I am saying this because of Charan.'

'Because of Charan? What are you talking about?'

'Yes, Charan Chauhan. About a year ago I was writing a script for him. He is a small time director,' Vinay explained. 'He had picked up the plot from a Munshi Premchand short story titled *Do Saheliyan*. You might have read it. He told me he wanted it adapted into a script. I thought it was a great opportunity. I burnt the midnight oil, toiled with office work and finished the script. I knew no one, no one knew me, I was a nobody. I was completely in awe of this person, he was the only one giving me an opportunity, a break if you can call it that. When I finished writing I gave the script to him. I never heard from him again. He said the project had been shelved and he was working on a new script now. He is going to release a new production soon. I bet it is the same script I had written, which he now calls his own!'

'I don't think Sagar is that kind of person,' I said in his defence. I had liked and respected him. He had given me encouragement and hope.

'I do hope he is not, but I thought the same about Charan for six whole months, I used to worship him, until this happened. I have read your script, and I personally think it's quite good. You are an innocent, sincere person. So was I. But I was taken for ride, isn't it? I learnt it the hard way. *Yahan koi saga nahin hai.* No one here is a friend, Sanjay. Each man for himself.'

Our auto had reached our destination. Sagar had told me he would be working in an editing studio in the vicinity, and had asked us to visit him there. Eleventh floor of a multi-storeyed apartment building in the heart of the Lokhandwala complex. Rent must be upwards of forty thousand. How much he would really be making to afford a place like that? I wondered.

'Come on in Sanjay,' Sagar said, opening the door. He looked tired and drowsy, as if he had not slept through the night.

'I was working on an edit all night long…don't mind if the place seems a little untidy. Can you guys take off your shoes there?' He said, pointing to a corner near the door.

'Oh that doesn't matter, Sagar. Sorry we've come at a time when you are in the midst of something and we are disturbing you. By the way, this is my friend Vinay,' I said, making the introductions.

It was a one BHK apartment with the spacious bedroom converted into a studio. It was sound proofed with large recording and editing equipment placed in the center. Neither Vinay nor I had ever been inside such a place and were most impressed.

'I thought I would never hear from you again,' said Sagar, 'you just disappeared. Where have you been all these months?'

'I am sorry Sagar,' I replied remorsefully, 'I know you would have wanted me to revert back to you a long time ago. I was just caught up in some other commitments...sorry, I can't talk about them, and therefore couldn't complete the script when you wanted it. I didn't want to come to you until I had finished *Nametag*. I did so yesterday, and here I am.'

I took the script from my bag and handed it to him. I had worked hard on it over the last few months, and as on that day, the eighty-two page document I held in my hands was the only reason for the smile on my lips. I had put my mind, heart and soul into it and I was satisfied with what I had written. I was confident it was a good script, and would connect well with the audience.

The conviction in my words would first have to be ratified by Sagar before it even got to the audience, though. I sought to impress him with my professionalism, sincerity and attention to detail. To this end, I had ensured that the script was presented in the prescribed format, the punctuation had been checked to the last comma, it was printed on white executive bond paper and spiral bound with a neat title page and cover. It looked handsome. So when I did hand it over to Sagar, it was like placing your precious baby in the arms of strangers, hoping they would love it and take good care of it.

Sagar immediately started riffling through the pages, taking a perfunctory look. He stopped at one of the pages that caught his attention and started reading, running his fingers over the words

Sameer

(holding the cup in his hand)
Thank you. Someday, Shalini.
(he says, pointing to the
congregation) I have to be there.

Shalini

(not paying attention)
Ya, ya, I know you will be. Accha listen, there is something very important I have to tell you.
(pause)
My parents have fixed my marriage.

Sameer

(perplexed)
Fixed, meaning?... What do you mean fixed?

Shalini

(nonchalantly)
They have found someone for me.

Sameer leans over. Looks into her eyes. Holds her hand. The voice beseeches.

Sameer

But...I love you. You know that.

Shalini

(looks at him, speaks defiantly)
I can't do this Sameer.

Sameer takes out a piece of paper from his pocket.

Sameer

I wrote something for you.
(tries to open the note)
I...I thought I would...

Shalini

(interrupts)
I don't want it. I don't want
anything. I have to go.
(pause)
I am sorry. What can I do? Don't be
sad. I can't bear to see you so sad. I have
to go.

'Nice', he said, smiling to himself, 'you see here Sanjay, this is conflict. This is what I was talking to you about that day.'

'Thank you Sagar,' I said, half blushing, 'I hope I have been able to justify the faith you had in me.'

'This is just one scene. I will see what you have done in the rest of the pages. Tell me, what is the premise of your script? Any changes from that short story? Can you break it down for me in brief?'

'The basic premise, the idea remains the same,' I said, 'but I have worked on the treatment. On the face of it, it's a love story. The protagonist loves a girl who can't love him back and is loved by a girl whom he can't love back. So the script is about the inherent intricacies and conflicts in their relationships. But I think what makes it memorable is the honesty and rawness in the characters.'

'Hmm' he said, thoughtfully, 'this is your first script right?'

'Yes,' I replied.

'It would have been better if you had come to me earlier Sanjay. I am currently working on another project. Don't know if I have time for this right now.'

'I…I can wait Sagar,' I replied hesitantly. I had no other option. I had to keep faith in time. I had to keep faith in the man. 'Whenever you find time to go through the script, do let me know.

I have in fact shifted to Mumbai now,' I said enthusiastically, 'maybe we can get together more often and take this further.'

'Of course Sanjay we can do that. Would you mind if I keep this copy here with me? I will get back to you when I have read it.'

'Sure Sagar,' I said. Vinay was nudging me from behind. He was concerned about something obviously. 'I had made this copy only for you, to read at your leisure. You can keep it for as long as you want.'

What goes around comes around, this is what the mothers in our homes and teachers in our classrooms teach us as we grow up. The lessons we learn from those moral science classes in senior secondary schools, visits to the temple on a Tuesday or a mosque on a Friday, words of wisdom that our ingrained within our uncorrupted hearts. Those who share never live poor. Share lunchboxes during the recess, share clothes and books with the sibling, share notes with the classmates, share ideas with humanity. A good word spread around never goes waste, a good deed never goes unnoticed.

Did I not fear that what Vinay had said may come true? I did. I was petrified to my core. That script was a fruition of months' of hard work and toil, my dream to see my creation on the stage, on the screen. But a man cannot live all his life with cynicism, can he? Faith and hope are what keep a person alive, and we latch on to them even when everything around us seems bleak. Do good and forget about it. Your trust might be broken sometimes, your spirit shaken, yet you hold on, keep faith. Keep falling and rising, keep trusting, keep doing the work you must do, day in and day out. And then one fine day when you least expect it, from sources unknown and unheard of, what goes around will come around.

TWENTY THOUSAND

For how long would you continue like this?

'This is an SRA building *saab*, ten years since construction. Don't come back later and say I didn't tell you that earlier. *Baad main koi lafda nahin mangta hai apne ko.*'

'SRA? What do you mean Prashant bhai?'

'*Arrey*, SRA meaning Slum Rehabilitation Apartments *re baba*. You English speaking people don't know English. Old construction, made for people who were living in slums earlier. Bambai is full of such buildings, and also of those jhopadpattiwallas. I don't know where they keep coming from every day. Bambai is now one big jhopadpatti.'

'So are you telling me I shouldn't take this?' I asked with some apprehension.

'Who am I to tell you anything *saab*. Water will come for two hours every day, and maybe never during the summers, there is a community tank nearby. Power cuts every week. I am an honest person, so telling you everything very frankly. *Baad mein koi lafda nahin mangta hai apne ko.*'

'Oh,' I replied, the word *'slum'* still ringing in my head. This must be something like those chawls we used to keep hearing about, I thought. 'Isn't there a better place you can show me?'

'Better? What are you talking about *saab*? Prashant bhai can show you a palace if you want, *akkha Bambai hai apna.* You say your budget is 4000, so I bring you here. Rent is 8000, *ek party aur dega tumko.* You can share it then. Twelve month advance deposit.'

It was a crowded neighborhood in Jogeshwari, one of the western suburbs of Mumbai. The apartment building he had brought me to was located opposite the police station, with a small, barely legible board saying Teacher's Cooperative Housing Society hanging on the wall. The building had no lift. We took the stairs to the fourth floor.

The apartment seemed to end before it could begin. One matchbox sized room, a tiny gallery and a tinier kitchen. The place was one-fourth the size of my home in Raipur and at four times the rent. Gangsters might have now deserted the bylanes of Mumbai, but it seemed that the city continued to extort *hafta* from its residents by way of monthly rentals. And the irony is, millions of people like me still craved to be extorted, searching for their identity in the crowd.

The walls had huge damp patches, having soaked up the previous day's rain, the first of the monsoon season. Naked wires hung along the hallway, water dripped from the taps. The owner had forgotten to put in a flush tank and I knew I would have to beg Prashant to get it fixed. One window opened into the central hallway, with neighbors enjoying unrestricted access to the inside when bored, unless I kept it shut twenty four seven. The second and the only other window opened on to the ocean side, giving an angled view of the shoreline in the distance, and letting the cool breeze blow in. Just opposite the window a short distance away another multistoreyed building had been constructed. Even though the wind managed to make its way through, the sunlight had been barred for most of the day, leaving more than three-fourths of the apartment in shadow. I stood by the window and closed my eyes, absorbing the convolutions of the maximum city, the unpredictability of the wind direction and the breaking of a new dawn in my life.

'I'll take it,' I said, 'but I don't want a roommate. I will rent it myself. I had decided to exchange nearly half of my salary for some private time and fresh air, both of which are a rarity in Mumbai. Even though a good roommate is equivalent to a good soul mate in an alien city, a bad one can be a cellmate with natural propensities to rob you of your time and space. I wanted to live alone and devote that time to theatre, rather than waste time in frivolous activities that were possible with an unruly companion.

'Any news from Sagar?' asked Vinay, when we met in Prithvi later that evening.

'Not yet,' I replied. I had called him twice since then, without receiving a response.

It would have been naïve to expect him to respond if he hadn't liked the script. Both of us knew we had to be patient, keep hoping and keep trying.

'Renting a place alone in Mumbai?' he asked, 'That's courageous, seems you will get a lotta girls home!'

'Nothing like that Vinay,' I chuckled, 'I just thought living alone will help in better focus and concentration.'

'Hmm, you will also need some endurance to go with that,' he said. It was evident he had endured. The good thing about Mumbai is that the city opens its arms to befriend you. It helps you find companionship even in your solitude.

'But this won't remain forever,' he continued after a brief pause, 'especially once you get married.'

I could sense an undertone of anxiety in his comment. I didn't want a dear friend to embark upon a new relationship with doubt.

'Tell me one thing Vinay,' I said, trying to put this in just the right words, 'do you worry that getting married could somewhere come in the way of your writing?'

'I don't know, maybe,' he said, staring at the ground.

'You are taking the right decision,' I said. 'This day today, we are full of ourselves. But times change before we know it. Everyone needs a companion to live through their lives.'

He nodded. We sat there without speaking, for some time sipping our tea.

'Any girl in your life?' he asked. 'Where is Seema these days? She keeps uploading pictures on Facebook frequently. *Ekdum babe ho gayi hai woh.*'

'Yeah!' It was my turn to nod. With a smile I continued, 'Don't know where she is though. Haven't heard from her since college.'

'We didn't really understand what happened between you guys. Everything seemed just right, we were so jealous of you.'

'I don't know, maybe it wasn't meant to be. And if it is not meant to be, it is not meant to be. It was for the better I think.'

'How come? You found someone else is it? You snotty little Casanova!'

'Not 'found' found,' I said with a sheepish smile, 'I mean, yes there is a girl, and I am crazy about her.'

'From where? IOC?'

'Yes, from IOC, she was my colleague in Chennai.'

'So what is the problem? You told her?'

'No, couldn't. I don't know how! Her parents want her to marry another guy, some family friend's son. And she can't break their heart.'

'And what about yours? Does she like you?'

'I don't know. Maybe yes, but just liking isn't enough, is it? What if she does like me but can't say yes to me? I don't want to screw myself again Vinay, you know that. It's too damn hard. If anything goes wrong, I will be left crying alone while she will walk over to that Puneet guy of hers, keeping her family happy and everything.'

'Where is she these days?'

'Right here, in Mumbai itself. But I haven't yet told her that I've quit IOC and moved here. We talk on phone or chat sometimes, but the last time we met was more than a year ago.'

'I don't understand one thing,' he said, 'is her marriage with this family friend guy, what's his name, Puneet right, fixed or something? Like is the date out or anything?'

'No, not 'fixed' fixed. Whenever I ask her about it, she says it's going on. It got delayed because this guy got a promotion and had to go to the States for a year. Raagini too moved to Mumbai on a better job and a higher pay. So their families decided to keep the marriage on hold for some time.'

'And she has no idea what's going on in your head?'

'I don't know Vinay, I don't have access to her head.'

'Do you have access to yours?' he sounded distinctly irritated. 'Do you even know what you want from her? I will dream about her, spend sleepless nights over her but I won't tell her. I will cry over her but I won't tell her. Even though she likes me I think and I am crazy about her I won't tell her. And why? Because I feel her father's random friend's random son might be thinking of marrying her some random day he returns from the States? What kind of nonsense is that!'

I didn't reply.

'Remember one thing Sanjay,' he said, the soon to be married, supposedly relationship stud advising me the loser on relationships, 'either get her or forget her.'

Vinay was a good friend. He meant well.

***

Raagini was working in the corporate office of a private equity firm in the Bandra Kurla Complex of Mumbai. It was a highly reputed firm and hers was a much sought after work profile – I was proud of her. I had called her one day and she suggested we meet on the weekend. She said weekdays were extremely hectic for her and even though she was working this coming Saturday too, she would try and get off early. I offered to pick her up from her office by seven.

The towering glass building I had walked into reminded me of the ones in IOC. I now worked in a ten by ten compound, where the only glass component was the door behind the shutter and the tumbler placed on my desk. I walked up to the reception and asked for Raagini. The receptionist looked me up and down before picking up the phone to call on the intercom. She asked for my visiting card which I didn't possess. She suggested over the line that some Sanjay person had come to meet Madam. She told me to take a seat saying that Madam would join me in a while.

The clock kept ticking away the hours, the minutes and the seconds. It was eight pm, and there was still no sign of Madam. I tried to call her on her cellphone but she didn't answer. I sat on the sofa, reading the magazines. With the weekend coming up, it is usually difficult to shut shop early, I said to myself. She will be out in a while. The receptionist soon got up and left. She said her sirs and madams could be here all night, but she had a family to feed. She asked me if I intended to stay or come back later, I replied I'd stay. She told me where the coffee vending machine was, and the loo.

'I am terribly sorry Sanjay,' said Raagini, holding both her ears with her hands, as she walked out of the office an hour later. 'Forgive me please, please, please.'

She was wearing a sharply striped shirt tucked into the skirt, and over it a classy blazer. The hair had been straightened and gelled to stay in place. The lower eyelids were marked by crisp eyeliner and the lips adorned by a maroon shade. The feet were shod in high heeled shoes. She looked smart and sexy.

'You are two hours late,' I replied. 'This is how you greet old friends in your city?'

'I said na, I'm sorry,' she said. 'Come I will make it up to you. No going home to change. Let's head straight for dinner. I am very, very hungry.'

We started walking out towards the road. I thought she'd grab my hand like she used to earlier. She didn't. I started looking for an auto rickshaw passing by.

'What are you doing?' she asked.

'Scouting for an auto. You don't plan to walk all the way, do you?'

'No, no, I mean,' she said, with one of those infectious smiles I could kill for, 'wait here, I have a surprise.' She asked me to stand where I was and started walking towards the other end of the building.

A few minutes later, the headlights of a blue mini hatchback flashed from the gate. It zoomed across the premises before halting in front of me. The windows rolled down and a honk resonated in the air.

'Care for a ride sir?' she asked impishly.

'When did you…?' I looked at her with amazement. 'This is wonderful, congratulations!'

'Thanks', she said, her hands on the wheel, 'just bought it last month. It was a dream come true, my own car!' she giggled excitedly.

'But I am not happy with you,' she continued, 'I tried calling you so many times last month. I wanted to share the news! Your phone was unreachable. Where have you been?'

'Oh,' I replied, 'I was ... I was involved with certain matters. There are several things I have to tell you as well. Let's sit somewhere, where we can talk.'

We drove towards Carter Road in Bandra. It was nearing 10 pm and on a Friday evening, the Mumbai night had just begun to roll. Couples staring into each other's eyes or locking lips, joggers and walkers with music plugged into their ears, families out for a stroll, bikers zipping around policemen on the lookout for the naive, the place had something to offer for everyone. We parked the car and started walking on the joggers' stretch, under the trees and along the sea. On one end of the stretch was a famous rolls and sandwiches outlet. There was also a fancy restaurant opposite it, but I wanted to avoid it owing to the weight of my wallet. We walked over to the stall and ordered two rolls – chicken for her and *paneer* for myself. She loved chicken and hated *paneer*. I wondered what she would have ordered in the restaurant had she been a vegetarian.

'How have you been?' I asked, biting into the roll while trying to prevent it from greasing my shirt, 'how's the new job?'

'Doing well,' she replied. 'Leaving Chennai did me a world of good I think. I was beginning to feel trapped in that place. Job is great here, it has just the kind of profile I always wanted, you know, equity research. IOC was fine, but it was corporate finance, this is better.'

'And quite hectic, isn't it?' I asked, with a hint of sarcasm, I hadn't yet forgotten my long wait outside her office.

'Yes,' she smiled disarmingly. 'It is hectic somewhat. But manageable, you know na Sanjay, commuting is the biggest pain in Mumbai. I have rented a place nearby and now bought a car. So that saves a lot of time and energy.'

'Nearby? In Bandra?' I asked, perplexed. Bandra was undoubtedly one of the costliest places to live in the city.

'Yeah, just a little distance from here. Near Pali Hill, the best part is it's a ten minute drive from my office. Do come over sometime. I live alone. It would be nice to have some company for a change.'

'Rents must be quite steep, isn't it?' It was spontaneous.

'A little on the higher side yes,' she murmured. 'But it's a good deal. A neat One BHK for 40k, semi furnished. I didn't have to buy a lot of furniture, so it helped.'

Forty thousand rental monthly? That's twice my gross monthly salary! I shuddered.

'Okay,' I said trying not to give away the thought in my head, 'that's great, nice job, good place, near to office, new car. I am really happy for you.'

'Thanks,' she smiled, 'what's up with you? Where have you been for past few weeks? *Eid ka chand*. You were saying you wanted to talk about something.'

'Yes,' I said, moving towards a nearby bench. Once we sat down, I started, 'You know how you always said I should pursue what my passion was, do what my heart asked me to do, to prioritize?'

'Of course Sanjay,' she replied, 'I remember that very well. You should listen to what your heart tells you to do. I have always thought you had what it takes to go all the way.'

'Well yes.' My face was flushed. 'I don't know. But nearly two months ago I quit IOC.'

'You quit?' she exclaimed. 'Why didn't you tell me earlier? Where did you join then? Where are you these days?'

'Yes, I was going to tell you,' I replied hesitantly, 'actually when I quit, I didn't really join anywhere else. I just quit because I didn't want to do that anymore.'

'So right now? You are doing…' she probed, gently.

'I joined an advertising agency called Creator Labs in Goregaon as a junior copywriter. And I am working on our theatre group. There are few leads, nothing concrete till now. I recently completed the script and gave it to Sagar. Remember *Nametag*?'

'I remember of course, the one which Sagar had asked you to complete but you weren't able to earlier. Any developments there?'

'Can't say anything as of now Raagini. You know how these things work. Need to keep trying, that's all.'

'I understand Sanjay, and I really appreciate what you are doing now.'

'Thanks. I knew you would understand.' I picked up her hand.

'For how long will you continue like this?' she asked.

I was puzzled by her question.

'Like this, meaning?'

'Don't get me wrong Sanjay, I wish you well. I always have. And I am very happy for you that you are finally following your heart. But you must have kept a time frame for yourself, haven't you?'

'Have you?' I flashed back, 'for how long would you continue with what you are doing?'

'Maybe till I get married. Maybe after that, depends. You know I have limitations Sanjay. Next month, I have to go back home. Puneet is coming. It's his birthday, my parents are saying I should come.'

I let go of her hand.

'What is going on with him these days?' I asked curtly.

'Nothing much. He is in the States. Sometimes we talk on Skype during the night. I force myself to, I have to. Let us see. Some of his relatives are here in Mumbai, *didi* and *chachu*. They are very good people. Sometimes I go to their homes as well. I have to do this Sanjay, I don't have a choice.'

Should I say something to her right now, I asked myself. Where did I, the pittance earning struggling writer compare with the 'States' returned millionaire professional? Where did I even stand a chance in the face of the status enjoyed by Raagini? What kind of parents would want to give their daughter's hand to a man who earned much less than her and had no guarantee for his future? Even she thinks I can't continue like this forever. Maybe she herself doesn't think that way, but her parents certainly would, and she knows that. But I can't set a time frame for myself! How can I predict the future? This is the life I have now chosen, no one forced it upon me. For all I know, I might have to continue like this all my life, and I would want to! Would she have said yes to me had I been in IOC? Or her parents accepted me then? It's best to forget her Sanjay, I told myself again. You have set foot on different paths now. She is never going to be yours, no matter what. Forget her, give up all feelings you have for her. They will hurt only you and no one else. She has come into your life only to go away. That is the truth, accept it.

BUSINESS SENSE

She had a different DNA

'Who is playing the lead?' he said, flipping through the pages.

'The lead? We haven't really decided on the casting yet,' replied Vinay.

'Then decide,' he said, handing the script back to us, 'I should have a face who can sell. How else will I get the audiences?'

'Mr. Goenka, sir, if you could read it once,' I pleaded, 'if it is good enough, it will get the audiences by itself. Why should we need a big name to star in it?'

He had a wry smile on his face, as if he had generous amounts of pity and sympathy apportioned for us, and for our naivety. He put an arm around my shoulder and started walking. Vinay followed.

'You have written the script, son?' he asked.

'Yes sir I have,' I replied, 'and I think we can stage it.'

'Hmm...I see. So if you don't mind my asking, what do you do for a living?'

'I work as a junior copywriter in an advertising firm,' I said.

'You are liking it?'

I didn't expect the question. 'Yes sure sir, it is quite good,' I replied.

'I used to work in advertising earlier,' he said, 'ran an agency. Those bastard clients, they don't understand an iota about advertising yet get to boss us around. No room for new ideas, no place for fresh talent. Don't tell me you don't feel that way? Don't answer that. Anyway, then I changed my line of business, ventured into production. I became the client myself, you know what I mean. I know showbiz, do you hear me? I have produced more houseful shows in this industry than the number of times you have heard the word theatre. Mumbai, Bangalore, Calcutta, Delhi, Chennai, Ahmedabad, Jaipur, all over the country. I don't need to *read* the script to know whether it's going to make money or not. It is instinctive, gut feeling. Have any of your works been staged or published earlier?'

'Not yet,' I replied, 'but there is always a first time, isn't it?'

'What's your background?' he asked.

'Background sir? You mean?' I asked hesitantly.

'You educated?'

'Yes, actually, a business management background. And an engineer prior to that.'

'And your friend?' he asked, pointing towards Vinay.

'Same background sir,' I replied.

'An engineer and a business manager should build bridges or sell soap, not waste their time with screenplays. You will never have the creative essence of art and literature,' he declared. 'Anyway, you specialized in marketing in your business management school?'

'I did sir.'

'So tell me, if you were in my shoes and a random guy like you walks up to you and asks you to stage his script, what would you do?'

'I will read his script,' I replied.

He laughed. 'You have read the script, and it's a brilliant script. Then what?'

'Then I will stage it,' I said. What was he trying to prove? I wondered.

'And who will come to watch it?' he asked.

'If it is a good play, then people will come once they know it's a good play.'

'Fair enough,' he replied, 'and how will people come to know if it's a good play before watching it in the first place?'

I thought I understood the first piece of the jigsaw puzzle he was prompting me to resolve.

'I will have to promote it,' I said.

'And how will you promote it?' he prodded further.

'Maybe I will put advertisements in newspapers or hoardings at street corners,' I said. I was not sure whether I would actually do this. It involved a gargantuan amount of money.

'And what will you say in those advertisements?'

I didn't have an answer to his question. I could say it's a remarkable love triangle with a refreshing treatment and is evocative but then there would be several others making the same claims as well. Why would people come and watch *my* play in the *first place*? That was the reason he was insisting on having a face or a name that would sell. I didn't have any. I needed a platform to be able to showcase my work without apparent commercial risk. My silence gave him the answer.

'I am a businessman, son. I mean well for you but I will only produce and promote your play if I see a return. You don't have the background to give me confidence that you have the ability to pull it off, you don't have any prior success to showcase, you don't have a name or a face associated with you which can attract an audience. And I must tell you making a production and promoting it involves huge costs. Why should I stage a production if I am not assured a profit from it? Risking my money on you makes poor business sense,' he concluded.

'Clutter breaking' and 'slice of life'– phrases often refrained in a boardroom clogged with clutter and devoid of life.

Ever wondered how it would be where an astronaut is taught space travel by a cardiologist, a cardiologist asked to operate on a four stroke engine, a garage mechanic's finesse gauged by how he hooks a cricket ball, a cricketer awarded runs by the way he grooves on the dance floor, and a song and dance competition judged by Mayawati? Advertising is one such profession.

It asks you to spread your creative wings far and wide and explore your limitations, yet be judged by the one man who has never explored them himself – the client. Even though that might be the irony which this art of business or the business of art feeds on, whatever the case that is, the client pays the money, and that settles the case. Goenka had learnt that very early in life. It's the greens that paint the world yellow, convert blacks into the whites, prevent the slips of the pink, and catapult the reds into, of course, the greens.

Suchitra and I sat in one such client's boardroom. A well known four wheeler manufacturer wished to prepare a jaw dropping advertising campaign for the upcoming festive season. Several concepts had been presented before, but the three wise men of the client team, the vice president, the category manager and the brand manager, didn't like any of them. There were huge sums of monies floating on the campaign and as the wise men put it, they wanted it to be 'just right', to rule the consumer's heart as much as the top line and the bottom line. Not satisfied with the concepts proposed by their contracted agencies, the ball had now been thrown in the open court and other, relatively smaller agencies like ours had been called to present their ideas.

'It has to be clutter breaking yaa,' said wise man no. 2, the category manager, with an exaggerated British accent he had borrowed from I don't know where, 'something unique that just breaks this clutter that we are going to face in the festive season. Everyone out there is going to shout about their own brand, each and every media vehicle is going to be cluttered, but we need to produce something disruptive that just breaks this clutter yaa, something which pops out of this clutter, you understand what I am trying to say?'

'And it should reach the consumer's hearts yaar, with a slice of life, that's what I want,' jumped in WM1, senior most of them all, with a Punjabi accent this time. 'Suchitra do you remember that recent advertisement for that famous chocolate brand?'

'The bus stop one?' she asked.

'Right *wohi*, see how it just touches the heart? Something like that, and then remains with you even after you switch off the TV and go for a walk. It should stick. I will give you an example,' he stood up and started walking across the room, addressing the audience. 'Anyone travelled in a roadways bus before?'

I raised my hand.

'In Punjab you know,' he continued, 'Punjab roadways bus with all the *sardars* and everything. There are towns located very close to each other, like Sonepat, Panipat, Karnal, Ambala etc. A new town after every half an hour.'

I nodded vigorously. I wanted to tell him it was Haryana and not Punjab, but decided against it. It was the import of his argument we were interested in, and I was the junior copywriter of a newbie firm and he was the senior most wise man amidst the three wise men, and the client is always right.

'Once when I was a kid you know, we were travelling in one of those buses,' he stated, as if it was the first and the last time he had travelled in a bus, 'and every time the bus would stop, some highway salesman would hop in to sell odd items. He would have not more than five minutes, but he had his sales pitch ready. In these five minutes, boss, he has to make an impact, convert a sale, collect his money and walk out. There was one guy I remember, this kid of some fifteen-sixteen years, as soon as he entered the bus and took his position, he made a disruptive, high pitched sound of a rocket being launched like a Diwali ka patakha, like shoooooooon,' he complemented his speech with the desired audio effect, 'and then announced in the same breath – Rocket *Kacchha.* I tell you guys, that young man sold ten underwear in five minutes that day. And even after some thirty years, the image of that boy hasn't faded from my memory.'

'Exactly, you understand what WM1 is saying?' continued WM3, the junior most of the lot, 'that's exactly what we want. Thank you sir. But at the same time it should also have relevance, it should add to the brand equity. We can't talk about a four wheeler and make Brazilian girls dance in hot pants all the time! Ours is a rational category. It is important to showcase the product, highlight the features and attributes very clearly and strongly.'

'So sir,' I raised my hand, 'should we make it emotionally appealing to reach the consumer's heart or rational to demonstrate the products' attributes or disruptive to break the clutter?'

'That's a puzzle for you to solve my friend,' interjected WM2. He was like the *manjhla bhai* of the troika I thought, acting as a mediator, 'but I don't want mediocre stuff, or something which has been done before, it should be fresh and innovative yaa. So let's get on to it, crack this in two days yaa,' he instructed, looking at WM1 for approval and WM3 for acceptance, 'let's now dot the i's and cross the t's.'

***

It was 9:30 pm on a Sunday evening. Orion complex in Goregaon wore a deserted look. I was pacing up and down on the pavement, rubbing my hands with anxiety. Suchitra sat on the porch nearby, looking up in anticipation. The dim light of the screensaver of her laptop flickered in the dark compound. Crumbs of the Domino's veggie extravaganza lay besides her, while she opened the black cola bottle and poured herself a drink.

'I would buy their vehicle if I saw this advertisement on TV,' she stated, 'it is relevant to the category and has a strong feel good factor about it.'

'Do you think the viewer will remember it once it vanishes from view?' I asked.

'I think so,' she replied. 'Sanjay you are being too apprehensive. I have seen and worked with several clients before, but in this case, their brief itself is very confusing. They want everything in their campaign at the same time, they contradict themselves. You can't have *makki ki roti* with sambhar and rasam no? It will ruin both the dishes and the meal altogether. No wonder they haven't been able to finalize an agency and a concept yet.'

'But you know how big this can be for our agency Suchitra.' I was emphatic. 'All we have done till now is print, outdoors and few pieces of digital. If we crack this, we break into the electronic media, the grass there should be greener. A future in mainstream advertising, a name in the industry. Do you think maybe, besides the three ideas we have finalized upon, we can also keep in reserve, one more presentation which is more entertaining? You know keeping the Indian audience in mind, throw in a little masala? They want something disruptive, so they just might like it.'

'I appreciate your enthusiasm Sanjay,' she said, 'but I don't want you to be overwhelmed by it. Just because this is a big client should we change what we believe in? It doesn't matter what colour the grass there is, what matters is the grass we truly want. It can be red, white, blue or orange, as long as it is ours, something we believe in and what makes us happy. It's not that I didn't have the opportunity to venture into electronic media earlier. I didn't do it because the client wanted something with regressive ideas, slapstick humor or unnecessary sexual innuendos. It might have been good business sense but not the right business sense. Don't worry about the name or the size or the profit and loss statement of Creator Labs, that's not our objective. What we want to do here is to create good, quality advertising. Business then, will take care of itself.'

Suchitra Dhani was not like the CEO of any other advertising firm fleecing clients on fake commissions and jacked up billing hours, she was like an artist who would work hard on every word or image until it satisfied her, as long as her work was ethical and had integrity.

The craziest thing was she didn't bother about winning. It baffled me, cause that was the sole purpose of life ingrained in me throughout pre-school, school, tons of extracurriculars, six years of college and now job. To WIN, to come first, always win within the comforts of our safety net. She had a different DNA. Sometimes she reminded me of Vishwant, but even though I had the highest regard for him, at the end of the day he was just an impoverished struggler, a status which even though I shared with him today, my middle class brain wouldn't accept for the rest of my life. At times she would make me aspire to the life being lived by Sagar Shah, but Sagar was an established name and successful in his passion, another outcome my middle class existence was unaware of.

We always live our lives worrying that if one follows their calling card only a select few can make it to the top, and by foolishly jumping outside our safety nets, we are not destined to be amongst those select few. Suchitra, on the other hand, was neither a poor struggler nor a successful select few. She was a middle classer like me who had carved out a life for herself out of her calling card. She had drawn happiness and a fulfilling existence from her passion, regardless of whether she won or lost, irrespective of whether she succeeded or failed. She would often quote the famous saying '*the race is long and in the end it is only with yourself*'. She was a living example of the same. She had free spirit, she commanded respect.

***

The first two concepts we presented got instantly rejected by the wise men. It seemed the client was determined to reject the preliminary ideas that came their way, no matter how good or bad they were. Men in advertising also learned the ruse with time, and would drag along few run of the mill ideas before coming up with the winner they might have up their sleeve. The skill here in the creative client face off is to identify the right time, when the client has satisfied his ego of rejecting ideas and is ready for approval. That is the moment when the creative needs to shoot the winner and get the nod instantly. The arrangement allows both the parties in the transaction to save face, appreciate the quality of brainstorming they had engaged in and come out victorious on the other side, patting each other's backs.

'Congratulations young lady,' said WM2, as he got up to greet Suchitra with a handshake, 'that is *"just right"*, the kind of stuff we have been looking for. It was a close call really amongst several agencies, but all of us have decided that this time we will go ahead with Creator Labs. Now don't let us down, it is one thing to think of an idea and a whole different thing to execute it to perfection.'

'And you young man,' he said, turning towards me, 'nice effort. Have you made any TVC before?'

'No sir,' I replied.

'Hmm…it would be better if you run the script by Dada today itself. He will be directing this, we must wrap it up in ten days yaa, need to go live by October first week, and this is September already. Suchitra, can you please send us the quote as well by the end of the day, include both studio and agency fees. Let's get going, people.'

***

Mumbai had been lashed by rain for three days now and it didn't show any signs of letting up. The streets were flooded, traffic paralyzed, and the railway network brought to a standstill. But a television commercial shoot once scheduled can't be postponed because of nature's fury. It involves a herculean effort to bring the whole unit together, from the celebrity to the client to the agency to the studio to the crew. The show had to go on. I walked into the gates of Mehboob Studio at Bandra at nine thirty in the morning. We had planned to shoot the commercial indoors because the weather forecast had predicted heavy rain. The prophecy that had indeed come true.

'Stage 2?' I asked the guard, adjusting the umbrella over my head.

'Straight, first left and then to the right,' he replied.

I stepped over puddles and walked around potholes. My house didn't have the luxury of a washing machine nor the facility to dry clothes in the sun. The continuous showers had made the situation tougher. It was an old and used pair of jeans and a crumpled shirt I wore that day, unable to iron it due to absence of power. There was water everywhere except in my taps, which meant this would be the third successive day I hadn't been able to bathe. I was ashamed of my disheveled appearance and hoped no one would notice the body odour despite the deo I had sprayed on.

Mr. Sudeep Deodhar, popularly referred to as Dada, was the director hired by the client to shoot this television commercial. He was a renowned name in the Indian Theatre and Film industry with several commercially and critically acclaimed productions to his name. Dada was busy giving directions on lighting and sound over the microphone to his crew who were at work preparing the set. I was told they had been there since six in the morning to prepare for the shoot. I walked over to greet him.

'Dada *namaskar*,' I said, 'everything ready?'

'*Arrey* Sanjay come,' he said, 'why so late?' He got up and took me over to the set. 'How do you think this is?'

'Come on Dada,' I replied, half embarrassed, 'you have designed it, it has to be perfect. Who am I to judge!'

'But you have written the script, isn't it?' he stated with pure professionalism. 'You must have a better idea in your head. Do you think the backdrop should be red or blue? What do you say?'

'Dada, I think that since the script involves the vehicle to be projected with the personality of the royal Bengal Tiger, the ferocity and energy of the animal could best be captured by the vibrations of red. The rest is up to you.'

'Ok,' he said, 'ya we can do that. Anything else you have in mind?'

Mr. Sudeep Deodhar, the revered adman, had appreciated and accepted my suggestion, *my suggestion,* no matter how trivial it might have been in the whole scheme of things. For me that was in itself like a lifetime achievement award. That by some strong coincidence or fate, he was today directing a script penned by me had just begun to sink in. When I joined IOC two and a half years ago, I could never have imagined that life would present me with such an opportunity. At that moment that day in Stage 2 of Mehboob Studios, for the first time I felt that somewhere amid the chaos my life was those days, I now belonged.

'One critical issue,' I said, 'the vehicle metamorphoses into the tiger in second frame and then goes back to being a vehicle in the fourth. How do we plan to capture that?'

'Come,' he said, leading me back to where his recording system was set up. He switched open his laptop and ran me through a few animations. 'These are the last three options we have zeroed in on, we might run the shot with all three once and then see what fits best during the edit. What is in your head?'

'I think the last one captures the theme most appropriately,' I replied, 'It has a gradual evolution rather than a sudden switchover like the other two, a transition that best reflects concept of the commercial and the brand thought as well.'

'Good insights, these, Sanjay,' he said, 'most copywriters I meet these days would have an anecdote in their heads converted into a script, most of them with buffoonery that captures eyeballs. As long as the client likes them why should I bother? But what you are coming up with is something well entrenched within your complete communication thought.'

'Thank you Dada,' I said with a modest smile. I felt somewhere in background my marketing experience was responsible for what I was saying. Steve Jobs was right, some dots do join backwards. 'Did you like this script?' I asked.

'As a matter of fact yes,' he replied, 'the idea is believable and appears to have come from the heart. Do you also happen to write anything other than TVC scripts or advertising copy?'

'Actually I do,' I replied, 'I have a strong passion for theatre.'

'Nice,' he smiled, seating himself on a cushioned chair kept aside specifically for the director, 'I myself run a theatre school for youth called Yuvaan. The objective is to give the youth an opportunity to express themselves. Pull up that chair, sit down.'

'I know Dada, I have heard a lot about Yuvaan,' I said. 'I know it gives budding writers, actors, designers, basically any young theatre enthusiast an opportunity to hone their skills and a platform to showcase the same. I wanted to ask you, could it also help in production?'

'Production? You mean commercially?' he asked, 'Yuvaan is more of a theatre workshop that teaches theatre to young talents. We do organize productions but they are more a reflection of the learning of the students rather than commercial scale productions. What do you have in mind?'

'I have written a script I believe in. I wish to stage it. But I am unable to find a producer willing to put his money on it. Everyone says since I am an unknown face it won't make good business sense. I also don't have strong leads in the industry that can give me a break.'

'I understand Sanjay but to be honest I don't think Yuvaan would be able to help you in that. The group or I can help young talents like you to fine tune their skills and provide the right guidance but not lend commercial support to stage a production.'

'It's not about commercial support Dada, only to get a platform. A platform that gives us an opportunity to perform, where we can showcase our work, receive unbiased feedback without the putting the promotional investment at potential risk.'

'In that case, why don't you try your luck in the Interlude theatre festival?'

'In what?' I asked.

'The Interlude theatre festival,' he said. 'It's an annual festival organized at Prithvi theatre showcasing several plays of different genres. The festival is spread over seven days with a different play performed each day. Six of the plays are acclaimed productions but the seventh one is usually an amateur theatre group exhibiting its talent. It's like a wildcard entry. Auditions are called and if a group promises a worthwhile production, it is given a chance to perform at the festival.'

'And at what time of the year does the festival take place Dada?' I asked.

'It is coming soon,' he replied, 'sometime in November. If you can, try and stage your play there, come for an audition. You get a platform to perform in front of the industry. The rest is up to what you can do. To tell you the truth, there is an acute shortage of good playwrights and performers in the industry today. It's not that there is shortage of talent, what is missing is honesty. Everything comes from the head, like programmed storytellers, nothing from the heart. If the emotional connect is missing, the shelf life of a play decreases by the day. If you have what it takes, the sky is the limit. We would definitely look forward to see your work.'

Staging a production by ourselves, without the support of an already established theatre group and zero sponsors was not easy. It would require time, money, actors, technical crew, costume, a place to rehearse, making arrangements for sundry goods and services, the list was endless. An established theatre group has all the infrastructure in place. We did not.

On top of it, for a production that was just hoping to find a platform, there would be no monetary returns. Which meant it was a sunk investment. But as Suchitra would put it, sometimes you don't do things just because they make business sense, you do them because your heart tells you it is the right thing to do.

If she had the guts, why couldn't we? *Don't worry about the name or the size or the profit and loss statement of Creator Labs, that's not our objective, what we want to do here is to create good quality advertising,* she had once told me. Our objective, therefore was to do theatre not just for success, it was to derive pleasure from our passion, to create good, quality theatre. Business, then, might just take care of itself.

The flip side of having a low paying job was that I had more time for myself. I could now put it to use for the production, which otherwise I might have frittered away in a weekend to weekend existence. If Dada could put that trust in me, there must be good reason for it. Sometimes when we are wandering hopelessly through a maze, the way out is right in front of us, but we don't see it, don't recognize it. It takes a stroke of inspiration to open our eyes to a possibility that seemed invisible till now. That is what happened when I met Dada that day – it opened my eyes to a whole new possibility, a possibility that had not occurred to either Vinay or me, until then. Staging a production ourselves for an audition at the theatre festival might not lead us anywhere and could be a sheer waste of time, money and effort, yet it seemed to be the first step in the right direction.

THREE CUTTING CHAI

It's about finding faults in each other,
it's about inspiring each other.

Vinay had got married. He had known the girl for quite some time and it was one of those cases where matrimony seemed the logical step forward for a mutually collaborative relationship. It was as much a decision governed by the mind as by the heart, and even though we had not yet stepped over his pre-nuptial anxieties about marriage interfering with his passion for theatre, I wished and hoped he was happy with his decision.

A senior secondary school teacher by profession, his wife Smriti had left her job in Delhi to relocate to Mumbai. Owing to budgetary constraints and readjustments that are part of every such significant event of our life, Vinay had now shifted base to another suburb further north of the city. Smriti was busy setting up her new home and in welcoming guests for the first few weeks. Today for the first time, she had accompanied him to our usual téte-a-téte at Prithvi.

'Have you heard of Interlude?' I asked Vinay, as the three of us sat down with our cups of tea.

'Interlude the theatre festival?' he queried.

'Yes, you know about it?'

'Of course I know about it,' he replied, 'it is one of the major theatre festivals of Prithvi. Goes on for a week, seven different productions. Last year, I even approached several theatre groups with a script, thinking one of them might agree to stage it. But it was the same old story, most of them refused, one of them did consider, but the director wanted to make several changes according to his whims and fancies, an idea I was not amenable to.'

'What if we don't approach any group or any director or producer?' I asked, my face brimming with child-like enthusiasm, 'what if we stage it ourselves?'

'Stage it ourselves? How? I don't think you can perform in the festival unless you are an already acclaimed production house or...'

'Maybe we can,' I cut him short, 'I met Sudeep Deodhar and...'

'You met Dada?' he asked surprised, 'founder of Yuvaan? How? Where?'

'Remember the TV commercial I had scripted? It turned out Dada was directing it. I met him during the shoot. He told me that one of the plays performed during the festival could also be a new, non-acclaimed production. They will conduct an audition first and if they like the performance it gets through to the big stage!'

'Yes I know that Sanjay,' he said in a patronizing tone, 'but even for that we should know some group in the first place that will include us and our script, isn't it?'

'That's exactly what I am trying to say Vinay,' I exclaimed, 'Why do we need to *know* a group or a sponsor, why not be that group ourselves, be the sponsor ourselves. Why not stage the production ourselves?'

'Are you mad?' he said exasperated. 'Staging a production by ourselves is no child's play. It's not like a college level production we used to do earlier, this is professional. A lot of things need to be taken care of, arrangements made...'

'I know Vinay,' I interrupted, 'but earlier you were alone. Now we are two of us. Don't you think we can pull it off? Why continue to beg for alms and wait for someone to rescue us when we have the potential ourselves? We have done it before, although on a smaller scale I know but by now you have also gained enough experience in the world of professional theatre to know how a group works. Don't you think so? And financial investment is a voluntary decision, this is just a proposal, not forced upon either of us. One thing I know is I won't be able to do it alone, I need you.'

I noticed Vinay throw a furtive glance at Smriti. He was not a money-minded person but he was married now and had greater responsibilities. Besides, neither of us earned a salary that was to boast of.

'How much money would it involve?' asked Smriti, addressing both of us. This was the first time she was taking part in the discussion.

'For staging a production,' said Vinay, 'the single biggest cost component normally would be rental for the auditorium.'

'Which in this case would be nil right?' she asked.

'I think so,' I said, 'after all they are going to take the auditions. They would offer a staging arena to do so. What else Vinay?'

'Next would be the rent for a practicing area,' he said, 'we would have to hire a place where we can do our rehearsals.'

'Taking it on the maximum side, how much?'

'Say we practice for thirty days,' he continued, 'one month rental could be anything between ten to fifteen thousand.'

'Let's suppose we only get something on the higher side,' I said, 'fifteen thousand.'

Smriti had taken out a pen and a paper. She made a list of requirements and the costs against each item. 'What else?' she asked.

'Technical design for lighting,' said Vinay, 'We would need a professional for that. In normal circumstances, when a group comes up to stage a production they would invariably have a light designer with them. Everyday rehearsals would happen without the lights. But last two days would be run-throughs with complete light and sound. That would need an auditorium. Since this is only for a practice run, it might not be a commercial one, the cheaper the better. Renting that would involve some costs.'

'I have an idea,' remarked Smriti, 'why don't we approach an educational institution for this? Most of them have their own auditoriums, and they are available for most part of the year. We would only need it for a couple of days right? We can ask them to rent it to us. It would mean an additional income for them and serve our purpose. From my Delhi contacts, I might know some people who could help.'

'Suppose we hire an auditorium for two days, what could be the cost?' I asked.

'We used to sometimes rent out the one in our school in Delhi for some function or the other,' she said, 'I think per day per hour cost could be around Rs 3000. It might vary according to the rates in Mumbai though.'

'Let's keep it on the higher side, two days, 5000 each, that would make it ten thousand. And suppose we also hire a light designer, how much would that entail?'

'That can vary according to the quality of the person we hire,' said Vinay, 'I might know a person who does this. He is new but knows his job well. Keep around ten for him.'

'Total expense till now is Rs 35000, what else?' asked Smriti.

'Costumes and set design,' said Vinay, 'Sanjay, how many characters do we have in *Nametag*?'

'Six in all.'

'Keep about one thousand for each, six thousand for costumes, and keep another ten thousand for set design. This is on a higher side, can be reduced substantially with some creativity. Next critical component is sound design. Someone needs to design background score plus we would need equipment like a synthesizer or a *tabla*, depending upon what he chooses.'

'I think I might know someone who can do this,' I said gleefully, thinking about Vishwant. 'He also owns the instruments. But we might get him just for the last three days, would that be enough?'

'It would be if he is good. If he can do the design in one day, then coordination with the actors shouldn't take much time.'

'That makes it 51,000 thousand in all,' announced Smriti. 'We have covered the auditorium, rehearsal space, lights, sounds, costumes and set design. Anything missing from the list?'

'We would need some props and make up kits,' I said, 'let me think.'

'I did a quick mental run of the script in my head. We might be able to get certain objects like tables, chairs etc. from within the auditorium. Few other things we will have to buy, or rent. Everything put together, I guess the expense would be around eight to nine thousand. Which now makes it a grand total of 60,000.'

We stared at the piece of paper lying on the table. This was our first business plan of a Theatre Production House. Initial Outlay – Rs 60,000, Guaranteed Return – Zero, Breakeven – Infinity. If I had been asked to gauge the viability of the proposition from a third person perspective, I would have wasted no time in shooting it down. Considering Vinay and I to be the initial promoters of this Unlimited Liability Partnership, if I may take the liberty to call it that, it meant both of us had to shell out Rs 30,000 each from our very limited pockets. Unlike the Hindi movies we had grown up fantasizing about, we had no super rich dads to indulge us.

Money changes color according to the circumstances a person lives in. Few months ago, thirty thousand for me would have meant six bottles of Jack Daniels. Today, the same amount meant four months more of legal license to rent a roof in the nation's most expensive city. I was a bachelor, he was a married man. For him, the significance of the number was twice as much. I thought I should suggest investing the whole 60,000 myself. I could use whatever was left of my savings, and this insane idea was a propagation of my insane head. Vinay though was a self-made man, and even thinking such a thought would have been grossly insensitive to his self-respect. He would either be in it fair and square with whatever he had, or not at all. If he had been a bachelor just like me, he wouldn't have batted an eyelid before taking the plunge. He was a man of purpose but he was not selfish, and his was a situation that demanded more prudence and mutual consent between him and Smriti. Both of us sat there in quiet contemplation.

'I know how important this is to both of you,' said Smriti, breaking the silence, 'money can always be earned again but an opportunity once let go doesn't always come back. I think we must go ahead with this. And Sanjay,' she now turned towards me, 'don't take me otherwise, but if at any point of time you think you need any kind of assistance from us, please don't hesitate to mention it. You are like family.'

I couldn't find any words to say to her. I gave her a warm smile and thanked her for her gesture. I looked at Vinay who was smiling back at me. If there were any doubts about Smriti's support we might have had earlier, they were all dispelled forever in one split second. Vinay was one lucky bastard.

'Keeping the expenses aside, we are missing out on the most critical element here,' he said, 'people. We would need a team – actors, director, costume designer, set designer, sound and lights artists, production manager, make-up artist and at least one person to handle backstage, to state the minimum.'

'Before you decide on anything, I have a suggestion,' said Smriti, 'this is going to be a project out of your regular jobs. You cannot afford to waste time waiting for people to come for rehearsals. As far as possible, the team that we form must be within your circle of people, one person might need to multitask, but each one has to be someone you can count on. I can't say about anything else but I know 'make-up'. That is one department I can take care of. Plus, I can handle the production. It will take some time for me to find a job here, so the one month I have I can put to organizing the production. What do you think?'

'Can't say no to madam,' I chuckled, 'what about the most significant element, the actors?'

'There are six characters in *Nametag* right?' asked Vinay, 'can you just mention them?'

'One male lead and one female lead, one male support and one female support, and two other support characters, both male.'

'You play the male lead,' he said, 'from what I remember you would fit best in that role. I am not very suitable for the male support but I think I can still play it, and it would mean one less person required. What do you say?'

'I say it sounds perfect,' I enthused, 'what about female lead?'

'What about your IOC girl? Can she act?' he asked.

'Raagini?' I exclaimed, 'she can very well act, in fact if I remember she was quite a theatre person in her early years before finance took over. I can ask her but she has a demanding job, I don't know if she would have time.'

'You go and ask her, I am sure she will make the time,' he said with a wink. 'And Smriti should play the female support.'

'But I don't know if I can act Vinay,' she hesitated, 'if something goes wrong, I won't want to screw this up.'

'Then let it go wrong Smriti,' he said, 'you asked us to find people we can count on. The actors are the most critical element of the production and we can count on you. In fact more than 90% of your acting depends on how you are directed, and we shall take care of that.'

'I think Vinay is right Smriti,' I said, 'anyway you will spend most of your time with us. Vinay will help you overcome any shortcomings that might be there. Which brings us to the most important question, who will direct?'

'Exactly,' said Vinay, 'first of all I think Smriti should not look after production. There are many things that will crop up as time goes by. She has not handled a production earlier. Sanjay, it is best that we choose between ourselves. One handles production and the other handles direction.'

'In that case,' I said, 'you should do the direction and I will handle the production aspect. My copywriting job allows me to sometimes work from home, I might be able to squeeze out more time than you can and hence run errands. Plus, if you handle direction you will have more time to train Smriti bring alive her character. Both of us will be there during rehearsals, anyway, so I can chip in with my inputs. But you better handle Raagini well!'

'Haha,' he laughed out loud, 'don't worry, I will make her fall in love with you in real life as well!'

'Who is Raagini?' interjected Smriti, 'am I missing out on something here?'

'No one,' I replied, 'I mean, she is a friend of mine, that's all. Lives in Mumbai and is good at acting. So as we discussed we'll see if she can play the role of female lead. What about the remaining two male characters?' I asked Vinay, trying to divert the conversation away from Raagini. 'They are both men in their late thirties or early forties. So we would need men in that age group who can take on those parts.'

'That is the tricky part,' Vinay replied. 'Arranging for young actors is still possible, but scouting for senior actors is a tough task. Even if we get some good artistes the challenge would be to bring them to rehearsals on time. We might even have to pay something, don't know how much. I know a few artists from some theatre groups, I will see if I can find someone. What about costume and sets? We would need a person with a design background.'

'And someone who can be counted upon,' emphasized Smriti.

'Design background! I think I might actually know a person who can do this,' I jumped with joy, 'Suchitra, my senior in Creator Labs, she is the Leonardo da Vinci of our times!'

'But would she be willing to join in?' he asked.

'Yes she would,' I stated emphatically, 'we can count on her.'

On that corner table of Prithvi Theatre, with three cutting chai and a dream, a team began to take shape. Theatre is all about team work. It's not like cinema where parts can be shot discretely and then all brought together in one single tape to be viewed a zillion times over. Theatre is live, with no scope for mistakes, no retakes or reruns. It requires a group of equally committed people passionate about their role, whatever it is and however small, determined to create a few moments of magic on the stage. Even if it means they have to rehearse, slog, curse, keep faith in the dream and perform together. It's about camaraderie, it's about pointing out faults in each other, it's about inspiring each other. Theatre is trust. You can be as good or bad a performer as your co-actor is, because it's about surrendering in trust. Theatre is an expression of every aspect of art and emotion, from literature to dance to song to design. Theatre is life in its most vivid forms.

We walked out of there that night with our jobs cut out. Vinay had to scout for the light designer and two male actors,

Smriti had to arrange for the props and make up kits and work on her acting, and I had to make a call to Vishwant, Raagini and Suchitra.

Vishwant agreed to my proposal instantly. He congratulated me and said he was very happy for me. He thought my taking the plunge was an inspirational act. I thought he was the one who had always been the inspiration. He said he would consider it an honor for him to be a part of our production. With all my heart I reciprocated the sentiment. Since he was still in Chennai, his only concern was the return air ticket to Mumbai, the key to which I knew was with Raagini.

***

The next weekend I went to meet Raagini at her house in Bandra. I hoped she would agree to the idea, not just because I held secret dreams of us being the next Saifeena, but because her being a part of the team would mean we got one actor we could count on and who we didn't have to pay. Few decisions in this world are made with both economic and emotional considerations, and this was one of them. But I knew how much she loved her job, how she was always more aware of her limitations rather than her passions, so in my heart I was sure she would say no.

It was around 1.30 in the afternoon when I rang the doorbell. She opened the door and her hands were covered in dough. Obviously I had barged in at lunch time. Thankfully, to make up for my unintended indiscretion, I was carrying a bouquet of flowers for her, for it was the first time I was visiting her home in the new city.

'I am sorry,' I said, 'I think I might have popped in at the wrong time.'

'Sanjay no, come on,' she smiled, 'it's all right, come in. It's a pleasant surprise! And it's a good thing you have come now, you can help me with the cooking. These flowers are for me? They are gorgeous.' She took the bouquet from my hands and placed them in a vase. She was wearing a cotton salwaar kameez without the dupatta.

'How come you are here today after so long? I thought you would come earlier. I told you I lived alone, and get bored on weekends, *kabhi to call kiya karo.*'

'I did think of that earlier,' I said, 'but during weekends I was occupied with struggling for leads. And then I thought you might not have time off from work, else you would have called yourself sometime.'

She must have noticed the sarcasm in my voice. She let it go.

'Leads for theatre?' she asked. 'Any developments?'

'All rejections mostly, but I, with my friend Vinay, have decided we will now stage the production ourselves. There is a famous theatre festival that happens in Prithvi during November, they call for auditions. We have decided we will perform there. I wanted to ask you for a favor.'

'That sounds good Sanjay. But what can I do?'

'You remember Vishwant in IOC? I don't know if you know this but he was a musician as well. I think it would be great if he could do the sound design for our production. Can you pull some strings to get him to Mumbai on a work visit sometimes?'

'That can be done,' she replied, 'I have good relations down there, shouldn't be a problem.'

'And there is one more thing,' I said tentatively, 'I want you too to be a part of it.'

'You want me to do theatre?' she laughed, 'it has been a long time since I acted in a play, I am not even sure if I remember how to.'

'I know you have always wanted to,' I said. I wanted to bring her back to the girl I had met during that dandiya night at Taj, the one I felt had gradually walked away from her own self. 'I remember, you said you felt everything around you was over. Maybe it isn't yet.'

'What did you say? So you have come to rescue me, is it?' she asked half laughing half angry. 'Is this a charity for the poor girl? I don't need your pity Sanjay.'

'It's not like that Raagini,' I hastened to explain. 'You are taking it all wrong. I want you to be a part of this. If there is anyone I would want to play this role, it would be you. Believe me.'

'But then why only me? You can find an actress anywhere.'

'Because I can count on you,' I said, 'it's the female lead in the play, *Nametag*. You read the story. You gave it to Sagar. You asked me to meet him. You encouraged me, you gave me the confidence. Today we have decided to stage it ourselves, I finally see some ray of hope, and I need you to be there with me. Please.'

'Why is it always about what you need?' she asked, her face turned away from me, looking out of the window.

'It's not like that Raagini, you know it's not like that.'

'And after that?'

'After that what?'

'I have to go home next month for a few days,' she said, turning towards me, 'Puneet is coming, I told you.'

'Why do you always have to keep preaching me but not do what you want?' I asked, 'You want me to follow my heart but you don't have the guts to follow yours. You keep telling me you don't have an option, may be you do. But tell me, do you really want to listen to what your heart tells you to do? Do you have the courage to accept it? If you don't like Puneet as you keep telling me, then don't go to meet him. What stops you from doing that?'

'I have limitations Sanjay,' she sighed.

'Do I not?' I asked her, 'do you think my life is a bed of roses? I am fighting fate out there. I am in that stage right now where I don't have any idea where my life is going… And I am telling you I need you, but I can't promise anything. And you know that, you have always known that. If you like Puneet and wish to spend the rest of your life with him, I am no one to stop you. I would want you to embrace and appreciate your new life with happiness. But not with resignation, not as a compromise, not with this fatalistic attitude. This is what you have always told me.'

'We begin rehearsals next week,' I said, 'I will wait for you. But don't come if you think you are being forced into this. Come if your heart tells you to. Come if you really want to be a part of it.'

Expectations reduce the joy in life, I had learnt. I expected more than what I could promise to Raagini, she received less than what she had expected. And both of us carried that burden on our heads. I went to meet Suchitra next, and she gleefully agreed to be a part of the production. No confusions, no mute understandings and no spoken misunderstandings.

I could say I trusted her, but even though I would not have acknowledged it that day, the truth was that I trusted Raagini much more than I could ever trust Suchitra. Yet, I would doubt Raagini's intent, mock her indecision and hurt her even though I didn't want to. The irony was, she too did the same. We didn't know how we had both brought ourselves to this place where we didn't want to be. We both wanted things to be as simple as they were when we had first met, when I took her to Taj and danced the dandiya. Today, we didn't know where the answers for both of us lay.

People come into our lives to go away, and we don't know why it was planned that way. If I had not been asked to follow the fine black print of Senduvan, if I had not been pushed into the darkest corners of my worst nightmares by Baap, I would have never found the courage or the perspective to question myself, or find the answers buried deep within my heart. I would have never picked up the shovel to dig the dirt away and unearth what I truly wanted to do with my life.

If I had not met Tiger Rana, I would have never realized the pointlessness of cursing one's fate, and if I had not met Ramteke, I would never have understood the sacrifice that following one's passion demands. If I had never known Vinay, I could never have brought myself to stick my neck out in the world, where now suddenly out of nowhere, missing pieces in my life's jigsaw puzzle were beginning to fit. Somewhere I could feel the riddle was beginning to unravel itself.

THE AUDITION

Fail as if we had never failed before

It was a standard V classroom in one of the primary schools in Andheri. We had pushed all the furniture into a corner to make some open space in the middle. Ram, one of the male actors scouted by Vinay was a middle aged service professional who wished to pursue theatre as a hobby. He was always on the look out for opportunities like this, where an amateur group would offer him an opportunity to perform. Also he took a keen interest in our experiment and didn't ask for money, but his only constraint was that he could come for rehearsals only after 9 pm.

The second member of the cast, Shyam, was a professional actor, and we had to shell out a lot of money to hire him. A professional light designer, Hari, and some equipment which had to be bought, inflated our budget estimate to ninety thousand. On the first day of the rehearsals Raagini had offered to chip in. We accepted her help gladly.

The classroom became available to us either before the children came in or after they had left. Once the children finished their Hindi, English and Mathematics lessons and the last bell rang, their blackboards became our planners and their benches our props. But our team could never be present together. Raagini could take time out of her job only during the mornings, Shyam could come late evenings and Ram only during the night. The good thing was that not all the scenes required all the characters at the same time, so we had to plan the rehearsals to be as mutually exclusive as possible. On weekends, we could get together for the whole day and collate the discretely evolved sets.

Vinay and I of course had no time off. We had to be the part of the process for each and every second. For almost six weeks, we had a twenty hour working day. I would wake up at five in the morning to reach the rehearsal venue by 6:30, rehearse for the play for nearly two hours before the school bell rang, go to office, attend to routine office work, get out from there by 5 pm, rehearse again till eleven at night, come back home by twelve, and complete pending day job deadlines by 1 am. If Vinay was held up in his office longer than usual, I would cover for him and vice versa.

Suchitra had given me the freedom to work from home, as long as I met my deadlines and didn't compromise on quality. The good thing about copywriting is it's an ideation based job, and an idea could hit anytime in those twenty hours, irrespective of my physical location. The good thing about Suchitra was that she understood and gave me that freedom. It would have been impossible had I been in a large multilevel agency. Suchitra also released me from long drawn-out client meetings unless my presence was absolutely necessary. She had taken those tasks upon herself. She understood what I was doing and why I was doing it.

It was the 19th of November, the day before the D-day – the day of the all important audition. The whole crew had gathered for a full costume, sound and light rehearsal. Ram, Shyam, Hari, Vishwant, Suchitra, Smriti, Raagini, Vinay and myself. It was ten o'clock at night. This was our third rehearsal for the day, continuous run time seventy eight minutes. We were all tired and hungry.

'Come down on the floor,' said Smriti to us sitting on the benches, 'all of you, make a circle and sit down here. I have a surprise!'

She walked towards her bag kept near the wall and took out two large casseroles.

'Home made khamman,' she announced, 'sit here in a circle and I will serve you.'

The word khamman made us all jump down and sit on the floor like dutiful schoolchildren. Ram, the forty two year old man and senior most amongst us was the first to grace the floor.

'Your wife is a very good cook, Vinay,' he remarked, relishing the pieces on his plate, 'why did you hide her from us for all these weeks?'

'To tell you the truth Ram,' Vinay said, half-smiling, 'this is the first time even I have been served the delicacy. Now you tell me who has been hiding from whom? I think we should get together more often like this, at least I will get to know what happy secrets Smriti has up her sleeve!'

'Do you want another serving or not?' threatened Smriti, apparently to Vinay.

'We should get together more often Vinay.' It was Shyam speaking up. 'I have acted in several plays before and while this too is quite a good one, what I have enjoyed most is the purpose you people have brought to the whole process.'

'I will have to shift base to Mumbai then,' chuckled Vishwant, 'Sanjay ji, *kuch jugaad lagao*.'

'Ask your madam,' I said, pointing towards Raagini, 'Ms. Raagini is the one with high profile contacts these days.'

Raagini's mouth was full of khamman. and she was not paying attention to the conversation. She pricked up her ears when she heard her name.

'What did you say Sanjay? Do you remember the Dandiya night in Taj? About two years ago, wasn't it? I think that was the last time when I had such delicious khammans. You remember?'

'Yes, yes I do,' I nodded, 'you danced less and ate more. I don't think anybody else even got a single piece that night, just like our fate today. Look you have already added one inch to the waistline!'

'Stop it, Sanjay,' interjected Smriti, 'don't talk like that. Those who live in houses of glass don't throw stones at others. First look at your own ever increasing waistline.'

Everyone was laughing like happy school kids.

'Ok fine,' I replied, 'make as much fun as you want. Hari, are you fine with the lights? We might get similar support tomorrow in the auditorium.'

'So far so good,' he replied, 'but this place does not have side panels and the dashboard is just four channels. If we can get a twenty four channel tomorrow or even a twelve one, I can create more variety with color and shapes and better control on strobing. The effects would really lift up our flashback sequences.'

'Prithvi does have both overhead and side panels plus a 24 channel dashboard,' said Vinay, 'but I don't know whether they would conduct the auditions in the main auditorium or the practice one in the building opposite to it. That place is not as well equipped as Prithvi is.'

'That is out of our hands anyway, isn't it?' remarked Suchitra, 'I think we have accomplished the best that is possible within the constraints of space, time and resources. Is there any stone left unturned Sanjay?'

'There is one,' said Vishwant, 'we don't yet have an identity. Shouldn't we give a name to ourselves? Like the name of our group or something related?'

'Everyone else is going to have the same stage, same lights and same facilities to perform with. Isn't it?'

'Remember what Goenka insinuated and what Sagar told you? We have always believed in our script,' he said, 'yet today, I don't know. I just...I just somehow feel we could have been better prepared, that as well I don't know how.'

'I know we might not be able to match a professional theatre group Vinay, but every professional must have been an amateur someday, isn't it? We have not left anything that could have been done. We have come a long way now, we can't go back,' I said.

'I am not talking about going back,' he retorted, visibly disturbed, 'and you know we won't be talking about this back inside. This production is as important to me as it is to you. You know what all I have given up in life for this? You had your claim to fame and glory while you were in IOC. For me, if I remove theatre from my life, I am a complete failure. I go back to my one room apartment where I try to run a family and my wife doesn't have enough privacy if guests come over, and I cry my eyes out. Do you understand? So don't you ever doubt my resolve and intent. Yet, it helps to have the right perspective.'

'I am not doubting you at all, Vinay, you are the last person I could ever doubt. It is your passion that encourages me, it is your resolve that motivates me, and it is your life that inspires me. I look up to you.'

'We are doing this for a purpose,' I continued, 'we have a reason for it. We have commitment, we have teamwork, we have our hearts and our souls in it. Let's not forget, we have finally got a platform we were so eagerly looking for. We love doing this, we enjoy doing this. That is what is most important, this is what I have learnt. You talk about my claim to fame in IOC

...I can happily swap one day of the past two months for all those days back then. What worse can happen, yaar? We will fail right, not be shortlisted to perform in this festival, fine, but no one can stop us from performing today, can they? Let us go out there and fail with joy. Fail as if we had never failed before.'

The clock struck seven thirty in the evening. The Fourth Wall will commence its performance at eight pm, it was announced. We had been given half an hour to set up the stage and ready ourselves. The previous group walked out of backstage to make way for us. Suchitra, Hari and Vishwant scurried towards the stage to set up the props, lights and sound system. Smriti and the rest of us went backstage to put on our costumes and make-up.

The judging panel comprised three people- two men and a woman. The woman was one of the owners of Prithvi theatre, one of the men was the chief sponsor of the festival and the other was an acclaimed scriptwriter and director. There were also few other notable personalities in the audience, Dada and Goenka amongst them. This must really be a Wild Card of considerable importance that these people had taken time out to watch the auditions, I thought. Tonight truly was an opportunity for someone from the wilderness to propel themselves into the limelight.

Lights went out. The curtain was drawn. The audience sat waiting. I took the mike in my hands and recited from behind the stage, the words echoing into the auditorium.

They tell me to seek what all I desire
The glory of Kings, the fame of Empires
The riches of land, the powers of fire
The stars of the sky, till I expire.

Yet all I need to live through this life
And all that I've craved for ages, tonight
For all I desire is the sound of your voice
For all I can die, is the look in your eyes.

Ladies and Gentlemen – The Fourth Wall is proud to present to you our first production – *NAMETAG*: **Have you found love?**

The curtains rose. Nine people, three judges, seventy eight minutes. One of the most memorable seventy eight minutes of our lives.

SEVENTY EIGHT MINUTES

The audiences chanted Encore, Encore!

'*Teen plate pav bhaji, do plate tawa pulav aur chaar plate aloo parantha*,' I said, as the waiter dutifully noted down the order. 'Add to that nine masala thumbs up, and make it quick!'

We had gathered at a beachside restaurant in Juhu, just after the performance. Everyone was famished, stomachs growling and crows cawing inside. Night had descended over the land. Fishermen's boats were finding their way back towards the shore. Our audition was over and the result was to be announced the next day.

'A toast to The Fourth Wall,' said Shyam, raising his masala Thums up into the air, 'Cheers!'

'Cheers!' we all responded.

'I think we did quite well,' he continued, 'apart from a few minute hiccups, it was a flawless performance. And going by the other performances today, I say we have a strong chance!'

'There are two more groups lined up for tomorrow,' said Ram, 'let's not get too presumptuous. But irrespective of what happens tomorrow, I had a great time with you all, and today's dinner is on me.'

Everyone tried to protest but Ram would not budge. He was the eldest in the group so the young gen acceded to his request.

'Especially the two girl stars, Smriti and Raagini, well done!' he continued, 'If I am not wrong, Raagini was acting after a long time and for Smriti this was a first, right? Sanjay and Raagini, what chemistry both of you had on stage. I must tell you, you were playing the lead and hence the most significant part of the play, and it was your intimacy that brought the whole plot alive. Otherwise, it could have simply fallen flat like any other mundane love story.'

'Thank you Ram,' smiled Raagini. 'Actually you will have to excuse me right now,' she said, getting up to leave, 'I have to be somewhere. And I might not be able to come tomorrow, do let me know the results as soon as they are announced.'

'Where do you have to go?' I blurted out, 'Stay for some more time na, till everyone finishes. It's getting late, we will drop you back.'

'No thanks Sanjay, but I really have to go, I will manage.'

She got up and started walking towards the road. Vinay nudged me from behind. I excused myself, and followed her to the street.

'Raagini!' I shouted, 'hold on.'

She stopped as I ran towards her.

'What happened? Why are you leaving so suddenly?'

'Nothing happened Sanjay,' she replied, 'don't worry. I really have to be somewhere right now.'

'Listen,' I said, 'I wanted to talk to you.'

'Then talk,' she replied coldly, 'what is it?'

'I wanted to thank you for being a part of the production, and also for contributing towards the expenditure. It was a big help.'

'You're welcome,' she said, 'I am sure if you had been in my shoes, you would have done the same.'

We stood there quietly for a few minutes staring at each other. After some time, she spoke again.

'Anything else? Or can I leave?'

'Yes,' I said, 'I wanted to ask you something. Did you go to meet Puneet last month?'

'Yes I did,' she said, 'and he is coming again next month. Our engagement has been fixed.'

'WHAT?' I almost screamed in disbelief. 'Your engagement? When, how?'

'You didn't expect that to never happen, did you?'

'No, I mean, yes, I mean, it would happen I know, but... so, as I had said earlier, I am happy if you are happy,' I said, regaining composure.

'I remember what you said that day Sanjay, and I thank you for that. You finally made me listen to myself. And that is why, I am not going home next month.'

'WHAT?' I shouted again. 'What do you mean?'

'I mean nothing,' she stated, 'I am not going for the engagement. I talked to Puneet last month when we met. I told him I didn't look forward to this marriage, and he won't be happy living with a woman who didn't love him. He is a good man, he understood. He had no other choice. I told my parents. They are not happy with my decision. They have gone ahead with the engagement anyway. Maybe Puneet will talk to them, maybe he won't. I won't be going. In some time they will understand. It is better they curse me for a few days than me cursing them for the rest of my life.'

'I don't know what to say,' I said, 'I am happy if you are happy.'

'There is nothing to say Sanjay,' she replied, 'but I want to thank you for everything, that's all. I don't know about the future but today I know I have made the right decision. I have no regrets. I won't accept life with a fatalistic attitude. This is what you have taught me.'

I don't know what love is, but that day, that night was a moment when we had helped each other find ourselves.

Even though we couldn't put it in words, we owed our lives to each other. Some things are not required to be said, they are to be felt and they are to be understood. It is important to respect the sanctity of every relationship, between every two human beings, and our silence that day was a mark of respect to what we shared with each other and would always continue to, irrespective of the turns the tide of time held in its hands.

***

It was a bright Monday morning. I couldn't remember when was the last time I had looked forward to a Monday morning as much as today. The sun had woken up in all its glory, the birds chirped away merrily. There was rhythm in the wheels of the train I boarded, there was laughter in the crowd through which I waded. The rickshaw wala wore a smile broader than usual, the traffic policeman danced to the signal. I hopped through the streets, skipping through the air. My dream is to fly, like an angel so high. I bowed my head to the guard at the venue, greeting him with a Namaste. The judges and participants had assembled in the auditorium; all seven productions were done with and results were going to be declared soon. Vinay and I squeezed our way to a corner of the last row. Before I had got myself entangled in the race of living for others, back in those days while I was in college and carefree, I remembered how I loved sitting in those last rows.

'All the productions we have witnessed in the last two days,' spoke up JM1, the judgeman no. 1, chief sponsor of the festival, 'have been exceptional in their performances. It is heartening to see that such vast oceans of talent and ideas exist all around us. Everyone here…'

'Yes, yes, we know, everyone was good but there can only be one winner. Come to the point sir, are we in or out?' the words echoed in my head. My anxious heart was skipping every other beat.

'Everyone here is a winner is what we believe,' spoke up JM2, the scriptwriter, 'the very fact that these groups came up here to present themselves makes each one of them…'

'Okay fine, we get the point. We know that. Now can we have the results please?' I pleaded.

'But as it is with life always, this year too in the Interlude Theatre festival, there can be only one wildcard entry,' said JW1, she who owned the theatre, 'and after long deliberations, we have decided that for the year 2011, the group that honours Prithvi for day seven of the festival, will be, The Fourth Wall.'

Disbelief! Ecstasy! Euphoria! I felt I was drowning. A swarm of people came up to congratulate us. We hugged each other, tears flowing down our cheeks.

'Be wary of being ahead of the times,' said JW1, 'this was just an audition. Your real test comes nine days later, when you face the real audience.'

'And don't miss out the opening ceremony and day one performance,' said JM1, coming up to congratulate us, 'you guys will have free entry for that night. Skip practice for one day but remember to come for the opening production. Good luck!'

It was a night of celebration. Even though this was just an audition and the real thing awaited us nine days later, it was one more step forward. JW1 was right, it is one thing being selected by a panel of three people, and a whole different ball game to be appreciated and accepted by an audience. We were yet to perform in front of them, the god of every artist– The audience. Every profession has an audience, every dream has a beholder through whom the dreamer fulfils the reason of his existence. For a doctor the audience is the eyes of a patient and the prayers of his relatives, for a scientist the audience is the next generation, for a lawyer the audience is justice. True men of karma live first for their own selves, and then for their audiences. There is a thin line that demarcates the two, a judgment that cometh only to those worthy of thee.

Two days later was the opening ceremony. Vinay, Smriti, Raagini and I had come for the same. The ceremony was followed by the first production of the festival. All the respected names of the industry were present in the theatre. No seats had been reserved. They sat amongst the audience wherever they could find a spot. We too adjusted ourselves in the fifth row from the front, towards the left hand corner. We had come in early, in an attempt to nab some good seats. We watched the auditorium fill in by the minute, hordes of people making their way in one by one. The stage had been set, the curtains were drawn. Seven days later, we would be there.

Within a few minutes, the lights were dimmed and a heavy baritone voice echoed in the auditorium.

Men and Women, young and old, beyond an age, beyond distances, beyond differences, beyond grievances, an emotion binds us all into one–Love. Love thy neighbor, love thy friend, love thy enemy, love all till the end. A saga untold ever before, a chronicle unheard by these walls and doors, The Galaxy Theatre group is proud to present to you, a Sagar Shah production – Love Beyond.

The audiences sat in rapt attention, who all came to act I need not mention
The curtain was raised, and the act was staged
One by one the sets were changed, the story unfolds, His ways are strange

Seventy eight minutes they sat in tight, I hear they said this is his night
They laughed and they cried, they were amazed and deprived
Lights shone on the floor, sounds echoed through the door
Shrieks of agony, pain and disgust, cries of joy, desire and lust
Loss of one is another man's gain, the circle of life turns wise men insane
Bravo! Superb! They chanted across, the hall was filled with huge applause
We can sit through the night, come on Once More, *the audiences chanted* Encore, ENCORE!

SECOND WIND

You gave me my second wind

It was a small, closed room. The one that had been used as men's backstage a few days earlier. A strong fluorescent bulb shone from the top, illuminating the whole room, not like a chandelier but more like an interrogation cell. At one end of the table nestled a large, wide chair, the kind usually reserved for the most important person in a board meeting. There was a sofa nearby, a couple of side stands that held old magazines, a painting of *Heer Ranjha* on the wall right behind the big chair and an old rug covering most parts of the floor, as if it was meant to make up for the dereliction of the makeshift setup. Two additional chairs were brought in from the nearby room and kept in front of the table and in the center of the room, where Vinay and I were asked to sit.

'You stole Sagar Shah's script,' said JW1, 'and presented it as your own!'

'This is unacceptable,' said JM1, 'and a serious offence. Such an act not only tarnishes the image of Prithvi but maligns the culture of Theatre.'

'Why did you do that? Why?' entreated JM2, 'I would still maintain I liked your performance, we all did. But why name a script as yours when it actually belongs to someone else? You could have said you are doing an adaptation right? Like many other groups did as well. Yes, you might not have got selected then because you scored additional points for originality, which we now know wasn't yours in the first place!'

We sat there quietly, our heads down. I was silent not because I didn't have answers to their accusations, I had a truckload of arguments I could have stated to prove the script was mine in original and copied by Sagar Shah, and not the other way round. They might not have listened to me, for I had no copyrights, the piece of paper which could have proven so. They might not accept it per se, but I knew they would have to believe me, I had conviction and I had no fear.

Yet, I didn't feel like speaking a word to them. I thought it didn't matter. What mattered was that I had let down Vinay. He had advised me, he had warned me, his apprehension was bred not by whim but experience. I didn't listen to him, and dragged him down with me to the grave. I was guilty. He had believed in me, stuck by me, supported me, helped me. But I had been selfish, I had been self-centered thinking only about my dreams and my hopes. *Nametag* was no longer just mine, it belonged to all of us equally, it belonged to The Fourth Wall, and even though in hindsight, I had no right to decide upon its fate by myself alone, by my own stupidity and adamancy. I was saddened and miserable. I couldn't look at him in the eye.

'I am sorry Vinay,' I said to him before the jury came in, 'I am sorry for what I did and I am sorry for what happened. I should have listened to you.'

'You are sorry for what?' he retorted, 'for giving your script to Sagar? I know I stopped you but at that time it seemed the best thing to do. We didn't know it would turn out this way.'

'But I should have listened to your suggestion, after what had happened between you and Charan…'

'A mistake yes, that is all it is. It doesn't take away from us what we have. The fact that we staged a production by our own selves which was appreciated and selected in an audition, it means something to me, to us. The fact that our script, not yours, our script won roars of applause in Prithvi. Okay, someone else presented it under his name I know, but we know it was our script, isn't it? And people loved it, the audience loved it. I felt I was the one standing on the stage tonight. I don't care what these people think Sanjay, I had never felt this way before. And I owe this to you. I had given up, I must admit. I thought I had failed and had nearly decided to quit. I was a pessimistic cribber when you came back to Mumbai. But when I saw you, I felt if this man can give up his security and comfort to relive what once was his passion, maybe even I shouldn't lose hope. You gave me hope again, you gave me inspiration. You gave me my second wind.'

He was looking up at me, smiling broadly. I think it was after a very long time I had seen him that happy.

'Sir,' he said, addressing the panel, 'ma'am, I know you think we stole Sagar's script, called it our own, made a production out of it and staged it in front of you to earn a place in the Interlude festival. If we had really done that, and had known Sagar was going to stage the same script tonight, would we have had the audacity to even come near to Prithvi the very same day? Or hope for you good people to allow us to stage our production here again? We would have been on the first plane to Italy by now, isn't it?'

'How do you think two nobodys like us would even have access to a script so decidedly preserved by Sagar, as was purported by his group tonight? How could we, who know nobody in the industry, have been able to sneak through one of his carefully secured works and even be able to stage a production in front of you before he could? You have all the right in trashing me for what I say, but is it not more feasible that few young passionate yet directionless men like us might have visited him, the acclaimed director, with our works to see if we could stumble across some kind of an opportunity?'

'Sirs and ma'am,' I now spoke up, 'The Fourth Wall came up to present *Nametag* to you because the group believes in its work, in its love and passion for theatre, it is with this drive that we staged the production that night. That is all, nothing else. You don't believe us, we shall accept your judgment, we would put trust in you good people and withdraw. Let Sagar take all the credit he wants for *Nametag*. We will come back again, with another script, not shared with anybody else, and present to you, to the audience of Prithvi. We can't always keep stealing stuff can we?'

The three of them looked at each other, none willing to speak.

'I don't know,' said JM2, 'we have a performance by the Wild Card group slated for seven days later. What do we do?'

'We can't have the same play to be staged again,' said JW1, 'that is out of the question. There is no way *Nametag* can be staged as the Wild card play now. What will it do to the reputation of this festival? People will ask questions, even if they are discreet, while some may shoot barbs in the open. I can't take that risk.'

'Lots of little stories you have up your sleeve young men,' said JM1, concluding the discussion, 'but the fact of the matter is that Sagar Shah has rights to this script, he is an acclaimed name in the industry, his production has been a super hit tonight and I am not going to put the blame on him just on the basis of some hollow claims of two random men I hadn't heard of until three days ago. Now as to what you say, well, part of that we might like to believe. But we won't, which doesn't mean that we believe in Sagar Shah either. You can have a little sympathy from us which means we are not going to take you to the court and this matter won't go outside these four walls. We are the ones who have known about your *Nametag* and we are the ones who know about Sagar Shah's Love Beyond. It is in your best interest that you forget you ever had a script called *Nametag*, it

Sanchit Gupta was born and brought up in the hills of Himachal Pradesh. He went on to co-found his own theatre group, worked as a radio talk show host, a freelance copywriter, an industry hopping brand manager and as content developer for a leading television network.

His first book – *The Tree with a Thousand Apples* – got long-listed at Sundance Screenwriters' Lab, Jio Mami Film Festival and Rabindranath Tagore Literary Prize. *India Today* called it 'Un-put-downable', *Aaj Tak* said 'Powerful and Beautiful', while *DNA* termed – 'Unforgettable'. As a screenwriter, he has written dialogues for Rajkummar Rao's *Behen Hogi Teri* while two of his written movies are currently under production.

When not writing, he is usually making travel plans with his wife or looking for people to play poker with. He says his works explore his fascination for global cultures, societal structures, vagaries of the world and the human mind, but you know that's all blah.

Praises for the *The Tree with a Thousand Apples* by the same author

'Has its heart in the right place'—*Saba Naqvi*

'Moved me deeply, it told me what every good writer says, there are no sides to take'—*Pritish Nandy*

'One of the best fiction works on Kashmir'—*Muse India*

'Bold and Riveting'—*Hans India*

'Fast paced, lucid and impactful narrative...takes you on a glorious ride and before you know, fills you with rage'—*Aaj Tak*

'Unforgettable'—*DNA*

'Heart-Breaking'—*The Citizen*

'The author, though not a Kashmiri, seems to have his finger on the pulse. He gets the intricacies and the tenor almost perfect.

It does justice to the big story that is "Kashmir". It is unforgiving, vivid, well-written, profound and well-paced for a debut novel.'

—*The Tribune*